The End Is Not Yet

Diane Pillars

This book is a work of fiction. Names, characters, places, and incidents are either products of the author's imagination or are used fictitiously. Any resemblance to actual persons, living or dead, events, or locales is entirely coincidental.

This book is not intended to replace the scriptures. It is not a learning tool. It is a work of fiction and, as such, is meant to be used only for entertainment.

The End Is Not Yet

Cover illustrations created by Dustin Pillars

Pillars of Publishing
PO Box 874023
Wasilla, AK 99687

Printed in the United States of America
First Printing, 2014

ISBN-13: 978-0-9903083-0-0
ISBN: 0990308308

ISBN: 978-0-9903083-1-7 (ebook)

DEDICATION

I wish to dedicate this novel to my husband Brian, my two daughters Tiya and Terrainna, my grandson Dustin, my sister Bonnie, and my friend Donnette for all their encouragement. Without them, after all the denials from literary agents since the novel was written in the summer of 2012, I probably would have given up trying to get it published. It was their little nudges that finally made me decide to self-publish it.

I would like each of you to know how much I appreciate all of the honest opinions that you have given to me. I love you all.

Most of all, thank you, Lord, for being with me every step of the way on this project. I pray that I have not blasphemed in any way in the creation of this novel.

ACKNOWLEDGMENTS

I would like to thank my husband, Brian, for putting up with all of the questions I asked him regarding the structure of the military, and for putting up with all my grumblings when things didn't seem to be going right.

I would like to thank my daughter, Tiya, for being so kind as to proofread my writing; she reread this book as many times as I had to rewrite it. Thank you to my daughter, Terrainna, for helping with a final reading that gave me the encouragement to move forward with my attempts at getting this published.

Thank you to my grandson, Dustin, for the lovely illustrations he created for the cover of my novel.

Contents

Chapter 1

The Beginning of the End

Brad and Debbie Porter felt it was their duty to vote in every election, to celebrate Independence Day, and to fly the American flag for all to see. They loved the life they lived on their Midwestern farm, and they loved the freedom that being a farmer in America gave them.

The Porters had two daughters. The older daughter was Tonja, who married Steve Philbig. Tonja and Steve gave Brad and Debbie three grandsons: Darren, Julius, and Troy. The Porters' younger daughter, Tasha, married George Fairer. Tasha and George were not so fortunate to have children of their own, so they made it a point to stay close to their favorite nephews. From the beginning, the families stayed close to each other.

They often worked together on different projects at each other's homes. They had big barbecues, went camping, and had family movie nights and game nights. Often a holiday get-together would be held on a day other than the holiday to accommodate one of the family's work schedules so that everyone could celebrate the holiday together.

Brad and Debbie had raised their two daughters to be kind, people-loving, and God-fearing. They were glad to see those teachings were being passed on to their grandchildren and great-grandchildren.

Brad and Debbie felt very fortunate to live in America. They were saddened when they watched the news and saw the plight of those in other countries. People were living in constant fear from their neighboring countries, and even from their own governments. They lived with disease and famine. They never knew if they would live from one day to the next. What was the world coming to?

The Porters respected authority because they felt that laws were put in place to protect the majority of the American people. They lived with feelings of comfort and safety.

Debbie Porter was small in stature. In high heels, she might have reached five feet, four inches tall. The wrinkles on her face were evidence of a difficult life. She had worked hard in many male-dominated jobs to prove that women were just as capable as men. She could operate heavy equipment. She was quite proficient in the use of guns. She could even kick butt at the billiards table.

Some of Debbie's male counterparts had scoffed and sneered at her. Had it been out of jealousy, or had they felt threatened by her abilities? It didn't matter. She would never admit it, but the negative comments did eventually take their toll. She retired early for a life away from it all, on the farm.

Now she was happy just to have a loving family and a comfortable home. When she had a moment to relax, Debbie loved to sit at her table with a cup of coffee and look out the kitchen window of their farmhouse.

Today she was thinking how beautiful and calm the water was on the lake that bordered their property. The bluff that stood like a crown on the other side of the lake was showing signs of summer. The snow that lingered on the ground between the trees was slowly melting. The birds flew as if they were just swaying through the sky. A cool breeze was coming through the window. *The snow won't last much longer,* Debbie thought. *Maybe a week or two at the most.*

She was starting to daydream about the past and trying to remember all the happy times. Her fears about the future took over. She wondered if humans were doing enough, and if there would be enough time to do anything about "it." *Something is going to happen. I can feel it in my gut and my bones. It will happen soon, but what will "it" be?* Debbie wondered if it would be a natural disaster, or possibly financial failures in other countries that would lead to financial ruin. *Could "it" be another country trying to overtake us or go to war with us? Or will it actually be aliens coming to earth, as some ufologists have predicted?*

Were aliens really aliens? What if our human ancestors had become so advanced that *they* built all those mystifying things that some believed could not have been built without the help of more intelligent alien beings? What if those more intelligent beings had actually been humans? What if they had been so smart that they were watching for signs of imminent doom, and they thought the world was going to self-destruct? Maybe plans had been made for some of them to escape—while escape was still possible.

The wealthy, or those of superior intelligence, were given passage on the spacecraft that flew away to safety. Those who couldn't afford passage, or were of lower intelligence, were left behind to fend for themselves.

The world, however, did not self-destruct, and those who had been left behind to fend for themselves did just that. They carried on, using some of the teachings of the more intelligent human beings. What they didn't know, they learned by trial and error.

Maybe those who had gone into outer space went to a safe planet, and their bodies evolved to adapt to life on that planet. All this time, they had been watching and waiting to make sure the world would be safe for their return.

They could not have foreseen that those left behind would become killers of their own kind, or that the stronger people would make slaves of the meek. They would not have guessed that humans would kill humans because of skin color, religion, or any other excuse. It would require an even stronger humanity to step forward and help the weak.

Is history doomed to repeat itself? Are we looking toward a doomsday? Will our more intelligent ancestors have to return to earth to help us defeat those who would annihilate us?

Suddenly Debbie's attention was brought back to the present. The TV was on, and a special message from the president of the United States was being broadcast.

He stated, "We are not at war, but now is the time to prepare and help other countries, so that we do not end up going to war.

"To every citizen of the United States: stop what you are doing. If you are away, return to your home. You must gather all of your excess food, fuel, guns, and ammunition.

"Your edible pets will also be used as food. Your money, silver, gold, and any valuables will be confiscated.

"The soldiers and state police will be coming to your home to collect everything. You will let them in. Anyone who resists will be shot. This is for the good of your country. Acts of defiance will be looked upon as treason, and every member of that household will be dealt with accordingly."

In her wildest dreams, Debbie never thought the end would start with an internal takeover. There was something eerie about all of this. She wondered if the country was headed for World War III. For some reason, the Bible came to mind. She pushed that thought out of her mind. After all, she had not been to church in many years.

The power went out. She tried to use the cell phone to contact her loved ones, but there was no signal.

Just then, Brad came in the door. Brad had always been her strength in the midst of storms. They were a match made in heaven.

Brad's stature was short, but his quick wit and strong shoulders and arms made up for that.

In any job, it had never taken him long to work his way up to a supervisory position. He was a natural-born leader. He would take into consideration the strengths and weaknesses of each of his subordinates before determining who would be placed in which position. Before making final decisions, Brad evaluated what the outcome would be for the worker and the company. He weighed all the pros and cons, keeping in mind that the company needed the worker just as much as the worker needed the job. Brad was always firm, fair, and consistent in his dealings with people. This gained him respect from both the workers and the company.

Brad was an avid reader. This helped him keep up on the newest ideas. In an emergency, he was able to act quickly because he would have already read up on the prevention and readiness techniques regarding the job or equipment that would be used. He also adhered to the trial and error and "get out and do it" attitudes. He knew what did and didn't work.

"Oh, Brad, I'm so glad you came home," said Debbie. "Have you heard the news broadcast? We need to try to contact the family. I've tried the phone, but it's not working. Do you think they shut down the grid to prevent families from getting together?"

Brad agreed. "I'm sure that's exactly what they've done. I'll take the Suburban and try to pick up those I can get to. You stay here in case anybody shows up. I'll start out toward Two Rivers, and work my way back toward home. I'll try to pick up Steve, Tonja, and Troy first, or make sure they're on their way. I will try to avoid going past any police stations, so I will be sticking to the side roads as much as possible. That might take a little longer, so don't worry if I'm not back soon. You start moving as much stuff on the list as you can into the hiding place. Put the dogs in the soundproof room first. That way, if anyone unexpected comes, they won't hear them barking or growling and give away the location of the bunker."

Debbie responded, "Sounds good to me. I'll get started right away. Darren and Cassie made an agreement with Jules, some time ago, to gather up all the kids first and then head out this way, in the event anything ever happened. I'm sure Jules will go there first to ensure they were able to pick up Paisley for him, and to help them in any way he can.

"Hopefully Charlene will allow Jules or Darren to pick up Paisley. This would not be the time for her to argue. I hope she's in a good mood. Maybe she will realize that Paisley is safer with Jules at this time.

"The kids will help me move as much stuff as possible when they get here. I hope we have stocked enough supplies to last us, for however long this takes. What about Tasha and George?" asked Debbie.

The End Is Not Yet

"I was talking with George on the cell phone when the phone went dead," Brad said. "He told me Tasha was working. She is probably on her way home. George, I'm sure, is loading up some supplies in their Blazer as we speak. He will want to head this way as soon as Tasha gets home, so he can avoid the cross traffic on the highway."

With that, Brad gave Debbie a kiss and set out to make the fifty-mile drive to Two Rivers. *May God go with him*, Debbie prayed within her heart. At that moment, she realized that she had often whispered little prayers or thanked God for this or for that. Maybe she hadn't really put the Lord aside. She just kept him hidden in her heart.

Debbie put the leashes on the dogs and headed across the field to the old abandoned barn. She and Brad had chosen the old barn to build the bunker entrance because no one would suspect it could house such a thing. The barn looked like a very dilapidated building that would fall over if a breeze came from the wrong direction. Inside a far corner of the barn was an old, half-collapsed toolshed. The boards appeared to be toppled every which way, as if they were rotting and falling off the toolshed walls. In reality, the boards were quite solid. The false boards made up the door that concealed an inner blast door. This was the true entrance to the bunker that soon would become their home.

The bunker consisted of a main room with a cooking area, an eating table, a game area, a large social area, and storage area. Along either side of the main bunker ran hallways with openings where three other bunkers were attached. With a total of seven connected bunkers, it was more of a community than just a bunker. Each connected bunker was built to house multiple families, with smaller cooking, eating, and storage areas in each. A person standing in the main bunker could not see into the other bunkers.

Debbie decided to prop open the bunker door. This way she could carry things into the bunker more quickly. Even with the door propped open, the bunker was still hidden, so it would be okay.

She would place the dogs in their special room. Then she would get the ATV up and running, and take it to the house to haul things. *Oh, I'm not thinking too clearly. I haven't grabbed any weapons,* she thought.

When she got back to the house, she needed to grab her handgun and make sure it was loaded. She revised that thought: She would gather all the guns hidden in areas other than the gun safe. She would ensure they were loaded. The gun safe could wait until there were more hands around to help carry weapons.

***

Darren Philbig was tall. He stood six feet tall and had a healthy physique. His chestnut-brown eyes complemented his enticing smile. His hair was receding a little too much for his twenty-six years of age.

In his early teens, he had pulled some dangerous pranks that had gotten him into trouble with the law. He did some time on probation. Now, even though time had passed, he still had to watch his every step. He had trouble getting jobs. People were leery when they met him, if they knew about his past. There wasn't, however, a more loving husband and father anywhere.

Cassie Philbig, Darren's wife, was cute. Her long black hair flowed when she walked. Her bright blue eyes sparkled when she laughed. She was tiny, but she packed a wallop. She was stronger than anyone expected. The phrase "backing down" was not in her vocabulary. Her compassion and encouragement helped keep Darren motivated. Without her, he would feel nonexistent.

Their two children had traits from both of them. Marty was seven years old but small for his age. He tried to act as if he was shy, but in reality he was quite the instigator.

Mary was four years old. She had her mother's bright blue eyes and her father's distinctive smile. She was called "the canyon kid" for the size of her dimples. Her hair was long and flowing like her mother's. It was sandy brown, with blond and red mixed in it. With her hair in ringlets, Mary could pose as a Shirley Temple doll. If you listened to her talk, you would swear that she was older than she was, except when she would get excited or try to say big words that she didn't use very often.

Jules Philbig was the exact opposite of his older brother, Darren. He was all of five feet, four inches tall. He took after his mom in that department. He was very muscular, though. His exercise of choice was lifting weights. His hair was dishwater blond. His eyes were incredibly blue. Their color, along with his long, dark eyelashes, made his eyes seem to smile. This tended to make people like him even before they had met him.

Jules was occasionally a bit short-tempered. If things didn't go the way he thought they should, he was either ready to fight, or was so put out that he was ready to give up. He was a lover of guns—any kind of weaponry—and muscle cars. He had to have the old muscle cars. He was a walking encyclopedia where cars were concerned.

Jules had had his share of bad luck with women, though. He tended to wear his heart on his sleeve, and that made him an easy target for the women he loved to try to control him. Jules was not one to be controlled.

He was the single parent of five-year-old Paisley. Jules loved his daughter so much that he tended to spoil her. Paisley, even at her tender age, seemed to know how to take advantage of this.

For the most part, Paisley was a good kid. She

was very polite and smart. Her personality would make her successful as a model or movie star. She loved to have people brush her long, almost platinum-blond hair. She knew how to speak with her eyes. From the way she looked at a person, they could tell if she thought they were being honest or were just trying to pull her leg.

"Marty! Mary! Gather up a few of your favorite toys, and get them in boxes now," ordered Cassie. She grabbed some food from the cupboards and placed it in boxes to be carried out to the car when Darren returned. "Hurry, kids. We have to go!"

In the meantime, Darren made the short drive over to Paisley's house. Jules had called Charlene as soon as he heard the president's announcement to get permission to take his daughter during this time of uncertainty. Paisley's mom was not so keen on the idea, but Jules was able to convince her that it would be easier for her to care for her other children if she had one less to worry about. The phone had gone dead while he was talking with her, so he would have to wait until he was able to contact Darren to see if she would allow him to take Paisley.

Charlene knew Jules would sacrifice his life for his daughter. Her present husband would not care as much about Paisley as he would his own children if things got to be really bad. She finally gave into the idea, and allowed Darren to take Paisley.

Darren gathered up Paisley and everything her mom gave him to take with her. There wasn't much stuff to gather up. Paisley was splitting time between her dad and her mom, so she had everything she needed at both places. Jules was now living with Brad and Debbie, so everything the two of them needed was already at the farm.

Darren drove back to his home to pick up his family and everything Cassie and the kids had gotten ready to take with them.

Darren and Cassie packed as much clothing, food, and supplies as they could get in the car. The kids were seated in the car with their legs propped on some boxes stashed between the seats. It wouldn't be a comfortable ride, but they could suffer through for the twenty minutes it would take to travel to their great-grandparents' house.

Jules pulled up just as Darren and Cassie were loading up the kids and the last of their stuff into the car.

"I'm so glad Charlene let you take Paisley for me," said Jules. "I didn't know exactly what was on her mind when the phone went dead. Thanks, Bro. I owe you a big one."

Paisley quickly jumped out of Uncle Darren's car and into her dad's car. She wanted to ride with her daddy. Seizing the opportunity to ride more comfortably, Marty and Mary begged to ride with Uncle Jules too.

The End Is Not Yet

They would all feel a lot safer after they got to Grandma and Grandpa's house.

***

As she got closer to the house with the ATV, Debbie could see an unfamiliar vehicle in the yard. Stopping the ATV, she decided to get a closer look on foot. She didn't have binoculars with her, so she tried to get as close as she dared to see them better.

There were more people than she expected to see at her home so soon. She thought they would be at their own homes, preparing for whatever the evening would bring.

These people were not the police, nor were they soldiers.

Debbie noticed a woman with a baby in her arms sitting on the steps. Two men were standing by the porch talking. She realized that one of the men was Darren. *That vehicle must be the one Darren told me he just bought,* thought Debbie.

She waited a little longer to see if other strangers were lurking around. Maybe she would be able to help Darren more if no one knew she was watching them.

Then Jules and Paisley walked around from the side of the house. Cassie followed after stopping momentarily to get some extra blankets from the car. Marty and Mary raced up to Darren to see who the fastest runner was.

Debbie could make out some of the conversations.

Jules asked Darren, "Who are these people?"

Darren responded, "I don't know. They were sitting here when I got here."

Debbie could tell by their demeanor that the boys were uneasy, but they were staying calm.

Darren shot Jules a questioning look and said, "They said something about a light leading them here. It disappeared just as they got to the house."

Jules tried to ignore that last remark "Where are Grandma and Grandpa?" he said. Not waiting for an answer, he turned to the man and woman and asked if they knew if anyone was inside.

The man said, "We arrived just before this young man came. We knocked, but no one answered, so we decided to rest for a moment on the porch. We thought he was the owner of the house."

Jules decided to look around, while Darren and the others stayed by the porch. Debbie decided this was the time to have her own look around. She would meet up with Jules when he got to the back of the house. This would keep her presence secret until she was sure things would be okay.

She met up with Jules in the backyard. They decided that she would go into the house through the back door and get some handguns—one for each of them, but not the unknown family. Jules would wait outside and keep an eye out until Debbie returned. Then they would both go cautiously around opposite sides of the house to the front to see if the situation had changed.

When they got to the front of the house, everything was as it had been. Darren was still standing and talking with the strangers on the porch. There was a soothing calmness in the air. The children were playing on the swing that hung from the tree in the front yard. The baby in the lady's arms was sleeping peacefully.

"I'm Debbie Porter. My husband, Brad and I own this farm," said Debbie, hopefully starting off the introductions.

The gentleman responded in kind. "I'm Harold James," he said. "This is my wife, Sue. The baby is our six-month-old, Shari."

Harold and Sue James was a quiet couple. They were used to going to their jobs, helping people, and going home. They were the type of people who went to church every Sunday, unless their jobs meant they had to do other things.

Harold was quiet but by no means shy. He spoke when he had something to say or could give some encouragement to someone. He did not enjoy hunting, although he loved to fish. He didn't care for firearms. However, his dad had made sure he knew how to use them, and use them accurately.

Sue was a very "girly" lady. She liked things frilly, neat, and tidy. She loved the icing on the cake. However, being a nurse, she could stomach a lot more than most people. She never squirmed at the sight of blood, and she could dissect things with the best of them.

Harold described how a light had led them to this doorstep.

As strange as it sounded to everyone else, Debbie knew it was possible. When she was in her late teens, she and her mother had gone shopping together. On the way home, they saw a light that seemed to beckon them to follow it. The light led them to her sister-in-law's house.

Debbie's brother was away from home on a job at the time. Her sister-in-law was feeling so depressed that she didn't know which way to turn.

The three of them prayed together. Before the night was over, Debbie's sister-in-law was feeling happy and revived. It appeared that she needed to know that others cared.

She had prayed about it, and God had sent the answer. *I wonder if these people are in God's plans for us*, thought Debbie.

Debbie felt no fear and sensed none from Harold and Sue. She asked, "What are your plans? Maybe you would care to join us. It appears to me that something sent you here."

"We don't really have any plans, per se," said Harold. "We just followed the urge to put as many supplies as we could fit in our vehicle, and follow that light. We really would like to join up with some good people. And like you said, something or someone sent us here."

The Jameses had left their vehicle hidden down the road in case soldiers came to collect things while they were there. They figured that if the soldiers took them captive for some reason, they didn't need to capture their supplies too.

When everyone saw their vehicle, they were amazed. It was a large covered truck. It was camouflaged. When Harold opened the back of the truck to show the type of supplies, Debbie gasped at the enormous amount of stuff packed in there. There was food and a lot of baby supplies, but there were also all kinds of medical supplies. She must have given them an odd look, because Harold promptly told her he was a physician and surgeon, and that Sue was a nurse.

The Jameses had known something was going to happen, so they had started stocking whatever they could. They had been praying for someone to join them who had the same thoughts about survival and companionship. The Lord knew Debbie had been praying for someone with medical skills to be able to join them, and here the individual was.

They all proceeded to haul supplies from the house and truck into the bunker. Brad, Debbie, and the family had already been stocking the bunker. That way, there wasn't so much to move when things did start to happen. They finally had everything moved into the bunker.

They rotated the supplies around so everything would be easily accessible, and they tried to put everything in a location where it would be used. They hid the truck and ATV in the woods as close to the bunker as possible without the vehicles being conspicuous. They covered them with camouflage netting and brush.

***

Troy Philbig, an average thirteen-year-old teenager, was running home as Brad drove by his house.

Troy was the youngest of Steve and Tonja's boys. He enjoyed the usual things that boys enjoy, such as camping, fishing, shooting guns, and computer games. On the other hand, there was a more sensitive side to Troy. He liked drama class, cooking, and joking around.

His sensitive nature seemed to make him more in tune with other people's feelings. Maybe this could be attributed to the age difference between the boys. There were ten years between him and Jules. Like all older brothers, Darren and Jules would sometimes tease Troy just because he was younger.

Troy, having been teased and knowing how it felt, never teased anyone younger than he, even jokingly.

"Hi, Grandpa!" Troy yelled to Brad as he saw the Suburban pulling up. He ran up to meet his grandpa, who was now standing beside the car door.

With a flip of his head, Troy swished his slightly long, sandy-brown bangs out of his eyes. "Mom told me to get my stuff together. I did that without question, so she let me take a break to go say good-bye to Jack. It will be hard for me not to see him for a while."

Troy, with his bubbly personality, normally liked to tease, joke, and laugh. Now he stood by his grandpa with a tear hanging from his eyelash. "I wish he could come with us," he said.

Brad, seeing the hurt in his grandson's eyes, said, "I do too, but we both know he will be better off with his family for now. I'm sure you will be able to see each other again soon." In his heart Brad was wondering how long it would really take for all this to blow over.

"Why don't you get all the dog food, dishes, leashes, toys, and whatever else you can find concerning the dogs," said Brad, "and start loading everything in the back of the 'burb? I'll go inside and see what kind of help your mom needs."

Troy started to walk toward the backyard. He stopped short and turned around. "Grandpa, what the president said about edible pets—he didn't mean dogs and cats, did he?"

"I don't know for sure, but it sounded to me as though he did. We'll just make sure our pets stay with us. They won't become food," replied Brad.

With renewed assurance regarding the safety of his dogs, Troy started to gather the items and put them in the Suburban.

Brad went inside the house. He found Tonja standing on a ladder, reaching for some dehydrated foods she had stashed on the top shelf of a closet.

Tonja needed a step stool for a lot of things she did. Her height of five feet didn't give her any advantage for being able to reach things easily. She had very tiny bones. Her eyes were hazel gray but would brighten to a bluish or greenish color depending on the color of clothes she wore. Her long brown hair fell down the length of her back and touched her waistline. She hated getting it cut, but if she was cleaning house, or if the weather was too hot, she would wrap it on top of her head in a heartbeat.

She was not as meek as one might think. A few years earlier, Tonja was hanging some laundry on the clothesline by the side of her house when she heard a noise coming from the backyard. It was a terrifying, growling noise. Then she heard Troy, who was only about eight years old at the time, let out a bloodcurdling scream. Something was after her son.

She saw a branch lying on the ground that had been broken off the tree by the wind the night before. Under normal circumstances, she would have barely been able to lift up that branch. With her mind and heart on the fact that her son needed her help, she lifted it easily and ran around to the back of the house to see what was happening.

As she turned the corner, she saw a black bear preparing to charge Troy. She lay that branch in front of her as a protective bar, and she moved between Troy and the bear. She raised the branch high overhead, as if she was going to throw it at the bear. She let out such a screech that it startled the bear. The bear turned and ran back into the woods.

"Tonja, where's Steve? Was he able to get home from work?" asked Brad.

"He's not here yet, but he called me just before the phones went dead. He left work when the announcement was made. Thank God for that.

"If he'd been just a little late leaving, he'd still be there. They closed the plant down. No one is being allowed in or out.

"He started riding the Harley to work about a

month ago. If anything happened, he thought he'd be able to get home a little faster than usual. He said he knew some shortcuts he could take with the bike that he couldn't with the car.

"I've got everything I can think of, so I'm ready to go. Shall we start loading? Troy went over to Jack's to say good-bye. I told him not to take too long."

"Troy's here. I told him to start gathering the dogs' dishes," said Brad.

Steve pulled up in time to help with the last of the loading. As he put their two dogs in Brad's Suburban, he announced, "Let's get going, before they close the highway down."

Steve had been listening to the news and talking with Brad and Debbie about something like this happening. He had been preparing for a day such as this. That was part of the reason he had started riding his motorcycle to work. The other reason was the economic value of doing so with gas prices being so high. He loved riding his Harley, and he was in heaven with such great weather to ride in. There was still snow here and there on the ground, but the roads had been kept clean enough for him to ride.

Steve was not a tall man, but he enjoyed working out regularly. He had a strong back, arms, and legs, as if he did farm work instead of the work he did at the plant.

Steve could be a leader, but he was just as happy

taking commands as giving them. He had no delusions of grandeur. He did what needed to be done, without any complaints. He was a true family man and enjoyed taking care of his family. That must have been where his sons, Darren, Jules, and Troy, got their love of children from. They would all lay down their lives for the ones they loved—and one day they might have to prove it.

As they arrived at the bunker, Brad noticed that George and Tasha had not made it yet. They should have been there before Brad had gotten home with Steve, Tonja, and Troy.

Brad said, "George and Tasha should have been here by now. I think I'll take a drive back to town to see what's keeping them."

Steve and Darren chimed in at the same time, "I'll go with you."

Jules and Harold decided they would stay with the rest of the families to help finish securing everything. They went back to the house with as many empty gas cans as they could get into the ATV. They were going to siphon as much fuel as they could out of the tanks of the vehicles in the yard. The vehicles would have to be left out in the open to appear as if they had been abandoned.

Jules said, as much to himself as to Harold, "We'll need all the fuel we can get."

Cassie, Tonja, and Sue watched the children and proceeded to set up the sleeping arrangements.

Debbie went back to the house to look around for anything they might have forgotten or might be of future use. *Bingo*. She had almost forgotten some seeds for when they could grow vegetables outside again. There were also some seeds that would do well under the grow lamps, providing the generators held.

As she passed the coffee table, Debbie grabbed the Bible that had been lying there like a centerpiece. She wasn't sure why she grabbed it, but when she picked it up, goose bumps ran up her arms and spine. She had not read the Bible in years, but somehow she knew she would need it now. They all would.

***

George Fairer, not being the type to wait, was loading up their Blazer. He wasn't impatient, but he was definitely not a procrastinator. He was actually very laid-back, but if he was going to do something, he would rather do it now and get it over with.

He had everything loaded up and ready to go by the time Tasha arrived home from work. The only thing left to do was grab the kennel and Sasha, their cat.

Tasha matched George in every way, even to the point that opposites attract. She stood about five feet, nine inches, while he was a handsome six feet. She had large bones as opposed to the tiny bones of her sister, Tonja. She had long, extremely curly hair. It fell to her waist when dry, but when wet and brushed straight, it reached down to her buttocks. George, on the other hand, had to keep his hair short to stop it from getting overly curly. Tasha had brown eyes to go with her blond hair, while George had blue eyes to go with his brown hair.

Tasha was a leader, and she had the smarts to go with that leadership. She always considered the consequences of their actions, while George would want to forge right in. She weighed the pros and the cons. In that respect, she took after her father.

Tasha pulled into the driveway, parked her Cruze, and jumped in the Blazer so they could get going.

Tasha asked, "Did you grab my vase?"

"Yes. I would never leave that vase behind," replied George.

He knew which vase she meant. A few years earlier, Tasha had been diagnosed with cancer and had to undergo surgery. Her fellow workers had taken up a collection and purchased a very unusual but elegant and expensive vase, which they had filled with a vast array of flowers.

She was now past her five-year cured date and was considered cancer-free.

The flowers had long since withered and gone, but Tasha had always proudly displayed the vase on a special shelf in her home. Every time she passed by it, it reminded her there was always hope.

After driving most of the way through town, George said, "Just a couple more cross streets, and we will be out on the highway."

As they passed through one intersection, they noticed the traffic was coming to a stop. They were about a half block from the next intersection. They couldn't see what was happening up ahead.

"I guess I spoke too soon," George said. "There must be a traffic jam up ahead. I guess we'll just have to wait for it to get moving again."

"I was lucky to make it home like I did," Tasha said. "The police were blocking off some intersections just after I had driven through them. I hope that's not what's happening up in front of us."

Meanwhile, Brad, Steve, and Darren drove back toward town on the back roads. As they got closer to town, Brad turned out the lights and continued driving on the side streets in the dark. As they pulled up to a cross street, they noticed a commotion about two blocks over at the traffic light.

Darren volunteered to sneak closer on foot to see what was happening, and to look for George's Blazer. So Brad pulled the Suburban over to the side of the street to let Darren out.

The End Is Not Yet

Darren returned shortly. "Sorry it took me so long. George and Tasha are in line about one and a half blocks away from that traffic light. I thought it would help if we knew what was happening. So I decided to sneak a little closer to the police to see if I could hear what was going on.

"The police have blocked the intersection so they can check all the vehicles for anyone trying to smuggle supplies out.

"They are making sure each vehicle is headed toward the address on the license of the driver. If the car is not headed toward that address, the police are demanding to know why the person is not complying with the president's orders.

"They are also making some of the people pull their vehicles out of the line. Those people are being loaded into government trucks."

Brad suggested, "Let's check the area for a way they can get out of line without being seen. We'll leave the 'burb here and search on foot. We'll separate and go in different directions. Hopefully, we will find an escape route faster.

"Try to keep tabs on each other in case one of us finds a way out for them. That way we can just use hand signals to get back to the 'burb."

Searching the backyards and driveways, Brad found a way for this to happen. He could see Darren, so he signaled for him to return to the 'burb. Darren could see Steve and gave him the signal to return.

Brad said, "I found a way, but it means George and Tasha will have to stay in line until two more cars move forward. If a police officer happens to glance in George's direction, all hell could break loose."

Brad told Darren, "Very cautiously, get to George's Blazer. Tell George to turn his lights off now, so it won't be so noticeable later. He needs to stay in the line and move up until he reaches the second driveway from where he is. Tell him to move very slowly. He is to turn into that driveway. Just before he gets to the garage, there is an opening on the left. There is also a tree there, but if he's careful, he can fit between the tree and the garage.

"He will then have to turn sharply to the right and follow down the left side of the garage. He will have to turn sharply to the right again, so he is going along the back of that garage. When he gets to the far corner of the garage, he will need to turn left. He'll have to drive over a small pile of garbage, but I'm sure he will make it okay. After he gets over that pile, if he just goes straight across that lawn, he will come out onto the next street over. If he turns left, goes to the corner, and turns right, he will see our vehicle. He will have to do this all without any lights. We'll be waiting for you. Stay safe."

The End Is Not Yet

Steve said, "I love you, son. Be careful."

"Dad, Grandpa, I love you both. Trust me. I can do this," Darren said.

About twenty minutes after they had come to a stop, Darren startled George and Tasha by opening the back door of their Blazer and sliding into the seat. He repeated the instructions Brad had given him.

All the police were busy checking the vehicles ahead. George was able to maneuver the vehicle out of line without being noticed. To help George after he pulled into the second driveway, Darren got out of the Blazer to guide them around the garage and out the other side of the backyard.

It seemed to take forever. Steve said, "I should have gone with him. It has been half an hour. He should be coming. It's only two blocks."

Brad replied, "No. If you had gone along, that would have given the police more opportunity to see movement. It was better this way. Darren is younger and more agile than we are. I trust he is using his head, and the excess time this is taking is because of the caution he is using. Like he said, we should trust him."

Those statements were bittersweet for Steve to hear Brad say. Things had not been good between Brad and Darren. Darren had had a wild side in his teen years, and had done some things his grandpa hadn't approved of.

Brad was a hardnose when it came to things like that. Brad believed people either toed the line, or were just no good. He simply could not abide anyone who would lie or steal.

Steve thought, *It is so good to hear Brad talk that way about Darren. This could be the start of a better relationship for them.*

A vehicle with its lights out pulled onto the street and moved slowly toward Brad and Steve. It was George.

"Let's get this rig turned around, and head for home," stated Brad with a sigh.

With Brad and Steve in one vehicle, and George, Tasha, Darren, and the cat in the other, they headed toward the bunker.

After arriving they found that everything was as it should be.

George and Tasha's supplies were unloaded into the bunker. The vehicles were parked by the house as if they had been abandoned. The fuel was siphoned from both vehicles as much as possible.

Tasha noticed Tonja and Cassie had lined some books up on some of the built-in shelves in the social room for all to read. She followed suit, and placed George's and her books there as well. Then she placed her vase on the shelf above the bookcase.

The doors were closed, and everyone was safe

inside the bunker. Jules rechecked the monitors for the outside cameras. He reported, "That was close. There are some soldiers driving up to the house right now."

Everyone stayed still and quiet. The bunker wasn't close enough to the house for any movements from inside it to be heard by the soldiers, but it made everyone feel safer just to be quiet.

All of the animals had been placed in the soundproof room, so no one had to worry that attention might be drawn toward them due to barking or noises from fighting or playing. It was a real miracle there wasn't any fighting among the animals. George and Tasha's cat had not been around other animals, and put up a real fight whenever other animals were around her or her home. But this time she behaved differently. She allowed herself to be put in the room with the other animals, and she just curled up and went to sleep, as if she was in the serenity of her own home.

Everyone watched as the soldiers ransacked the house. It was as if they were angry because the family hadn't left any food or supplies for them to confiscate.

What they didn't know was that some of the stuff they were breaking and tossing out the doors and windows were valuable antiques. Many were family heirlooms. With each item, Debbie felt a knife go deeper and deeper into her heart. She felt the knife twist and twist until it broke, and the tears that welled up in her eyes started to fall down her cheeks.

Her family looked at her and put their arms around her. Harold and Sue, by now, felt like part of the family. Seeing Debbie's pain, they put their arms around her too.

Suddenly it was as if the family heirlooms didn't matter anymore. The family heirloom was each heart entwining with one another. They were a family—working, living, and fighting to stay together and survive.

This really was the end of an old way of life. From now on, they would all be learning as they went. They would try to remember the teachings from their ancestors about how best to survive without modern conveniences.

They would be making new heirlooms.

Chapter 2

Vengeance in the Air

The first few weeks went by smoothly; but as time passed, one could sense the frustration everyone was feeling—especially the younger adults. They had never had to stay cooped up in one place for so long. They were torn between this being the safest place and secretly wanting to go out to see what was going on outside. It was hard enough for the elders to adjust to this imprisonment, but they knew they were safer in the bunker than anyplace else, at least until things settled down a bit.

The children were being very whiny.

Paisley snapped, "Mary, you can't touch my dolls anymore. I told you to leave those clothes on her, and you changed them."

Mary countered, "You need to share. I let you

change the clothes on my dolls. I want to change the clothes on your doll. You can't just tell me no!"

"Yes I can. It's my doll, and you can't play with it anymore."

Mary suddenly grabbed Paisley's hair. "I'll show you."

At that point Darren and Jules stepped in to break it up. Jules snapped at Darren as Darren took hold of Mary's arm. "It's about time you take control of your daughter."

"Mary doesn't act like this without being provoked. If you didn't spoil Paisley so much, maybe she would get along with other kids better."

Without warning, Jules jumped at Darren, and the fight was on. Cassie grabbed Mary's arm and yanked her away, just before Darren's leg flew past Mary's head. At the same time, Tonja pulled Paisley out of the way as Jules fell backward. Steve took hold of Jules, and Brad blocked Darren from trying to land a blow.

Steve, with all the authority he could muster, stated, "I don't understand you boys. You are the adults. We are in a situation here, and we don't know when it will end. You are brothers, and you need to act like brothers. You know you would lay down your lives for each other, and you may just have to before this thing is over. Your enemies are not each other. It is our government that is trying to take everything we've all worked for. Save your energy to fight them. Hold onto the love you have for each other. Right now you need to be examples for your children. I suggest you make up and have your kids do the same."

Darren and Jules relaxed, so Steve and Brad let go of them. They shook hands and gave each other a hug. Then they turned their attention to the two little girls. They were crying.

Jules reached for the doll Mary had been playing with, and gave it to Paisley. "Paisley, you need to hand this doll back to Mary, and apologize for being rude and selfish."

With tears lingering in her eyes, Paisley asked, "But Daddy, do I really have to let her play with it? She changed her clothes after I told her not to."

"Yes, Paisley, you do have to. She was playing with it. You like playing with her dolls. She has never told you not to change their clothes. That's part of playing with dolls—dressing them the way you want to. You enjoy expressing yourself that way, don't you?" Paisley sheepishly nodded her head. "Well, Mary does too. Being closed up in here, we all need good ways to express ourselves. It will help us enjoy the here and now a little bit more."

Paisley took the doll and walked to Mary. Placing one hand on Mary's shoulder and handing her the doll, she spoke softly, "You can play with my dolls anytime. You can change their clothes any way you want. I can change their clothes the way I want when it's my turn to play with them. I'm sorry, Mary. I want you to always be my friend."

Mary, wiping the tears from her eyes with her fingers, responded in kind. "I'm sorry too. You can also play with my stuff. We will be friends forever."

With her eyes brightening from an idea that popped in her head, Mary said excitedly, as if nothing had happened, "Wanna color?"

"I'm glad that's over," Debbie said. "I think we need to come up with more ways to use up some of this pent-up energy. Anyone for doing exercises together? We could make up a routine that would incorporate everyone's specialty exercise. Hmm, I can just imagine what that would look like."

Everyone chuckled.

"What's for supper?" asked Brad.

"We can use the last of the garden veggies for a salad. We still have a couple of roasts that seem to be lasting okay. I'll cook up one of those. Our fresh meats, potatoes, and squash will be gone by next week. If not eaten, they will be spoiled by then. We will be totally on freeze-dried, dehydrated, and canned foods after that," stated Debbie. "Tasha has started some tomato plants under the grow lights, but it will be a while before they produce any fruit."

George interjected, "There hasn't been any

movement outside this past week. Maybe the immediate danger in the area has passed. Do you think we could possibly send a couple of us out to scout the area? Maybe there is still some fresh food in the surrounding homes. Maybe we could get an idea about what is happening out there."

Brad responded, "It's an idea. Let's think on it over supper. We'll discuss a plan after we eat."

After supper, the ladies cleared the dishes and tended to the cleanup. The men remained at the table to discuss a plan of action.

Brad started off. "This will be our first attempt outside. I don't want anyone going off half-cocked. You all stay calm. Keep caution as your number-one priority, and we'll all come home safe."

It's hard to think of this underground dungeon as home, but home it is, thought Brad.

With some hesitation, Jules muttered, "You know, Grandpa, maybe Darren and I should be the ones to go out and have a look around first. I hate to say this. Not. We are younger and faster." This brought a little laughter from those that were listening. "We're both good with guns. Maybe we can take a quick jaunt around to see what we can see, and report back with what we find."

George piped up. "That's a good idea," he said. "Until we know what's out there, the fewer of us who go out, the better off we will all be."

Steve said, "I'd feel better with at least one older person going along. Seeing as I have been working out regularly, I think it should be me." Turning toward Darren and Jules, he added with a joking tone in his voice, "After all, we just witnessed how uptight you guys are."

The young men took the ribbing in good humor. They knew the incident was over, but laughing at it would help to alleviate any leftover tension.

Brad nodded. "I can agree with that. Remember, just have a quick look around, and come back. If you're not back here in one hour, we'll come looking for you."

Steve, Darren, and Jules made themselves ready to go. Tonja checked the security cameras for any movement outside before they opened the door. They gave last-minute hugs, and they were out the door.

It was a cool night outside, with a slight breeze. They worked their way around trees and brush, using them as cover. Soon they were by one of the neighboring farms. Everything seemed quiet and normal. It made them wonder what they were doing cooped up inside that bunker.

Just then, they saw a movement by the neighbor's shed. They all went down on one knee. This way they were as low as possible, but still had the ability to see what was happening.

There was a man crouched by the far corner of

the shed. He appeared to be hurt. Jules and Darren wanted to creep closer to help him, but Steve stopped them.

A small group of soldiers came around from the front side of the house. They were overturning large barrels, beating the bushes, looking around hay bales that were stacked in the yard, and checking the inside of an old automobile. They must have been looking for the injured man.

After waiting to see if any more soldiers were coming, Steve took command. "We need to try to help this guy," he said. "If the soldiers are after him, he can't be all bad. Darren, you head off to your right. Jules, you take the left. I'll get in as close as I can from here. I'll try to draw the soldiers' attention in my direction. Find a good-sized rock you can throw. When I whistle, we'll all throw the rocks at the same time. Aim for whichever soldier is closest to you. There are four of them, so get your gun up and ready as soon as you let the rock fly. We don't want to shoot unless we have to. If we have to shoot, be careful of cross fire, so we don't shoot each other."

After everyone was in place, Steve made a bristling noise with some brush to draw the soldiers' attention. Then he whistled.

To the soldiers it seemed as if rocks came from everywhere. One soldier was hit in the temple and died instantly. The other two were knocked off their feet. As they regained their composure, they raised their guns and started shooting wildly into the darkness. The fourth soldier was stunned at seeing the rocks flying toward them, but he composed himself and started shooting along with the others.

The time it took for the soldiers to start shooting gave Steve, Darren, and Jules enough time to take careful aim. With one shot each, they took the three remaining soldiers out.

Coming together at the scene, Jules remorsefully stated, "As many times as I said I would, I never really thought I would ever kill someone."

Steve patted Jules on the shoulder. "We can talk about that later. Right now let's go help that guy. We'll have to take him back to the bunker so Harold can take a look at him. We can't leave him if he's hurt."

As they got closer to the man crouched by the shed, he became more familiar. It was Paul Johnson, from up the road.

Paul Johnson loved farming, hunting, and fishing. He believed in taking care of his family and keeping them fed the best way he knew how. He didn't believe in fighting. He had been in the service and had seen enough fighting in Desert Storm. He wanted no part of war.

Paul had always been a strong-willed man, but looking at him now, it was as if all the strength had been drained out of him, and it wasn't just because he was hurt.

Darren asked, "Paul, what happened? Where's your family?"

"I was hiding in my basement." Paul's eyes started to tear up. "Bess and little Joey were with me. They found us, and they took me outside. I thought they were going to try to get information from me, and then let my family go…but they didn't. They didn't even get started on me. As they were dragging me past the basement window, I saw one of them slit Bess's throat, and then Joey's. He was only two years old. Why would they do that?"

Darren could see Paul's anguish and wasn't sure he wanted to hear any more. "You know, you don't have to talk about this right now."

Paul ignored him. It was as if he had to continue. "At first I just wanted to die. They started to beat me, and I let them. Then I decided I was going to live through this, and I would get as many of those bastards as I could to avenge my family. I waited for the moment when I could get the upper hand. I let them think I was getting weak.

"The soldier who was beating on me told the other soldier to go help with the scrounging. He said he could take care of me, so the other soldier left.

"The one that was beating me must have gotten

too tired. He had been leaning over me all the while he was pounding me. I guess he was making sure I wasn't going to get up.

"Then he stood up, as if with pride, and pulled his gun out of its holster so he could finish me off. When he stood, I tripped him with my leg. He fell, and I got the gun. I shot him.

"One of the soldiers in the house must have looked out the window when the shot was fired. As I was getting up, he shot me through the window. I tried to run but could only get this far. I'm losing quite a bit of blood."

Steve said, "We need to hide those bodies somewhere. It will give us more time to get back to the family and prepare to defend ourselves."

Jules suggested, "Dad, why don't you start back to the bunker with Paul? Darren and I can hide the bodies, and catch up with you later."

Steve admitted it sounded like a good idea. If they all stayed to hide the bodies, Paul would have to wait. He couldn't afford to lose any more blood.

When they got back to the bunker, Sue spread a sheet on a table in the medical supply room. Paul was laid on it, and Harold went to work on the wound. About forty-five minutes later, Harold was finished. He reported to Brad that he had cleaned the wound as best he could. Paul had been shot in the backside of the upper thigh. The bullet had exited through his buttocks.

The End Is Not Yet

Harold stated, "He is sleeping now. All we can do is give him a little something for the pain, keep the wound clean, and let him rest. He won't be doing any sitting up for a while. Sue will make him up a bed in our area so we can keep a close eye on him for a couple of days."

"Thank you, Harold," Brad said. "Thank you too, Sue. We are very lucky and happy you were led here to be with us."

Darren told the rest of them what Paul said had happened to his family. With heavy hearts at having heard of such a thing happening to their friends, they went, one by one, to bed. Sleep, even poor sleep, would be needed to keep them thinking clearly. They would need to be alert, now more than ever.

Jules sat on his bed, not wanting to go to sleep just yet.

Steve noticed this and decided to have a chat with his middle son. "Jules, you did a good job tonight. What you boys did tonight took courage. It takes courage to stand up for what's right and to help others, even if it means hurting the people causing the problem.

"You fired your weapon because they were firing at us. If those soldiers had caught us, we would be the dead ones. Believe me, they would not have been nice about it, or quick to do it. Then they would have continued on, until they found our families and killed every one of them, including little baby Shari. You did the right thing. We all did.

"Now try to get some sleep. When those soldiers are found, they will know some of us are still in the area. They will start a massive search. We will have to be ready."

The next morning, everyone except Paul arose early. No one really wanted to talk.

Paisley was the last to wake up. Her long blond hair was a mess. Some of it fell in different directions, while some of it stood straight on top of her head.

Brad decided to have fun with her. "Hey, Paisley, having a bad hair day? Maybe you should go back to bed for another twelve hours until it straightens itself back out."

Grinning from ear to ear, mostly because of the attention she was getting, Paisley responded, "Oh, Great-Grandpa." She climbed up to the table and asked, "Can I have some cereal?"

With that, the mood of the entire group seemed to change. The morning once again became its usual rowdy time.

Paul woke up around 9:00 a.m. He was seething with hatred.

"I want to get as many of those so-called 'good for our country' jerks as I can get. I'll be better in a couple of days, and I will be ready, willing, and able to go out on any escapades you guys want. I never believed in using weapons to defend my home before this. I always felt things should be settled peacefully, but now you can sure bet I feel differently."

Sue, sensing his feelings of despair, suggested, "Why don't you rest some more? You'll feel differently after a few days."

Paul countered her, "I may calm down, but I will never feel differently. Just imagine if you had a child murdered right before your eyes. You'd feel the same way I do.

"I still have some food and supplies at the house. I also have some hunting weapons and ammo that I hid when this thing started. Now I will use them for hunting real animals. I wasn't able to get to my stash when I needed it, but we can sure get to it now."

The pain was getting bad again, so Sue gave him another dose of pain medication, and he fell back asleep. He was still muttering that he would live to see this thing through, and avenge the death of his wife and son.

Harold asked Steve, "Did you hear any news about what is really going on out there?"

"We ran into Paul before we even had a chance to check any other homes for supplies," responded Steve. "I was hoping to hear some news from Paul. I guess we'll just have to wait until he wakes up again. Maybe he will be more rational and able to tell us more."

"Troy, what do you hear on the radio?" asked Cassie.

"Nothing. Absolutely nothing. It's as if no one is broadcasting."

George said, "The government is probably not allowing any radio broadcasting. They want us to come out and show ourselves. They want us to find out what is going on, so they can shoot us as deserters."

Brad stated, "If they only knew what true patriotism was. They'll find out before this thing is over, though. There have to be others like us out there. We'll just have to try to find them."

Debbie prayed aloud, "God, please be on our side."

With each day that passed, Debbie thought more and more about the Lord and the Bible. She started to remember things from her past that had long been forgotten until the family was forced to move underground.

When she was seventeen, her father died from cancer. Family from out-of-state had to stay in their home during the time of the funeral, so she and her two sisters had to share a bedroom.

During the night they were awakened to see a soft, light-blue haze at the foot of the bed. It was as tall as, and in the shape of, a man. It was not a reflection from anything in the room or from the window. It wasn't scary. She wondered what it was and what it was doing there, but it didn't frighten her. It kind of made her feel safe. It gave her hope.

Remembering the events that had happened in her lifetime when times were rough made her wonder why she ever stopped showing her love for the Lord.

She thought, *Is God trying to tell me it is time to start standing up for what I really believe in? Oh Lord, are we coming to the last days?*

The next day, they decided to go out again. Hopefully this time they would be able to gather some information about what was really happening in the country.

"A small group worked out pretty well yesterday. Maybe we should try that again," suggested Brad.

"I would like to volunteer to go out this time," said George.

"I would like to go again," stated Jules.

Steve suggested to Jules, "Maybe it would be better for you to hang back in the bunker for a day or two."

Jules almost snapped at him, "I can do this." He realized what that must have sounded like. He adjusted his tone of voice to a calmer one and continued, "I really want to go out again, Dad.

Everything will be okay."

Steve had confided in Brad what had happened the night before.

Brad interrupted the two. "Okay, Jules, but you will need to keep yourself in check until you know how you're going to react in situations. If I tell you to do something, I want you to do it without hesitation," Brad said. "The worst thing you can do is get out there under pressure, and then freeze when we need you most. I want you to stay right by my side."

"I'll do that, Grandpa," declared Jules.

"It's settled, then. George, Jules, and I will be the ones to go this time."

They armed themselves and left the bunker.

They decided to head north this time, figuring they might run into a few more people if they headed toward town. They had only travelled a few miles when they saw someone dash into the trees ahead of them.

"I'll try to flush him out from behind," George said.

With a nod from Brad, George started moving around the trees and tried to sneak up behind whoever was trying to hide from them. Brad and Jules crouched and waited to see if the person would come out in their direction. They soon realized it wasn't just a "he" or "she." It was a "they."

Brad and Jules stood and aimed their rifles at the people. Brad and Jules had no intention of shooting them. They just wanted to scare them enough to make them halt and talk to them. The people stopped abruptly when they came face-to-face with the rifles.

"Good work, George," Brad said as George came up behind the three people he had flushed out of hiding.

Brad, turning his attention again to the three people, asked, "Where are you from? Haven't seen you 'round here before."

The woman looked frail. It was hard to tell if she was weary from their ordeal or if life had done this to her. It seemed as though she was having some difficulty making decisions. She didn't seem sure what she should and shouldn't tell them. She couldn't decide if they were trustworthy.

The girl that clung to her side was also frail, but in a different way. She seemed slightly mentally deprived. She appeared as though she was in her early teens, but she was actually around nineteen years old.

The young man, on the other hand, gave an impression of arrogance, as if he actually ruled the household. His eyes said he believed he was the best, and no one could win in a fight against him. He was meant to rule, rather than be ruled.

"We are the Williams family," responded the lady in a modest and kind but shy tone. "I am Esther Williams. This is my son, Earl, and my baby, Madelyn. The soldiers killed my husband. We are from Chicago.

"I was shopping when the announcement was made for everyone to return home. I was almost home when I saw Earl and Madelyn running toward me. Earl told me the soldiers had killed their father.

"When I tried to go back home to see if there was anything I could do to help my husband, I saw some state police drive up to the house.

"Earl told me he had seen them kill his father, and there was no way he was still alive. There was nothing we could do, so we left without trying to retrieve anything from our home. We were hoping to find others we could stay with."

Lowering their rifles, Brad, George, and Jules each introduced himself.

"Rest assured. We have extra room, and I'm sure the rest of our group would be happy to have you join us," Jules said, looking at his grandpa for approval.

Brad responded in kind. "Yes, that's an excellent idea. You are welcome to join us."

"Thank you," Esther said. "I don't know how we will ever be able to repay you, but we'll try."

They all went back to the bunker.

The End Is Not Yet

Everyone seemed to bond rather well with the newcomers over a nice, warm dinner shared by all. Sleeping arrangements were made for the new family, and life continued as if the new family had been with them all along.

In bed that night, Debbie confessed to Brad, "You know, I really enjoyed talking with Esther. She's a very nice lady. And Madelyn sure liked joking around with Troy. But I must say, I have a few reservations about Earl. There is something about him that gives me the willies. I can't put my finger on it. There's just something strange and creepy about him."

Brad responded, "You know, I kind of have an odd feeling about him too. Maybe it's just because we don't know him. Madelyn is a little slow. It's possible that he feels the need to be overpowering because of her.

"We could be sensing his uneasiness. It could just be the inkling of it that is giving us an uneasy feeling about him."

"You're probably right. Anyway, time will tell, so we might as well get some sleep. I love you." Debbie gave Brad a kiss, yawned, and turned over on her side to go to sleep.

"I love you too," mumbled Brad, half under his breath, as he drifted off to sleep.

Chapter 3

The Building of Strengths

A careful watch was kept on the security cameras for any signs of soldiers.

Brad stated, "You guys must have hidden those bodies pretty well. No soldiers have been snooping around outside."

Darren said, "We buried them in the ground under all the cow manure piled up behind the barn there. We thought the manure smell might cover the smell of the decaying bodies if it started to seep up through the ground. Hopefully it will mask the smell enough to confuse any dogs the soldiers might decide to search with."

"So that's what that smell was when you came back. It was gross," Sue said as she scrunched up her nose as if she could still smell it.

Jules suggested, "Maybe we should go out and

try again."

Tonja, Tasha, and Cassie were having quite a conversation of their own in the corner by the sink.

Tonja turned to the men. "If you go out again, we think we should be included. This is our fight too, ya know. We can shoot just as good as any of you guys; and if it is just a scouting expedition, we would like to get outside too. We could be extra arms for carrying back more food and supplies. If it turns out to be more than just a scouting expedition, well, we are ready for that too."

Debbie interjected, "Sue and I can watch the kids and keep up security here. Paul can help too, if it becomes necessary."

"That would make a band of nine of us out there," said Brad. "That might be a bit much. If we run into trouble, though, it might take all nine to get us out of it. We could actually cover a larger area if nine went. I guess the pros outweigh the cons."

"What about me, Grandpa? I'm good with guns. You know that," Troy said with enthusiasm.

"Not this time, Troy. You stay here. We need you to help Grandma and Sue keep this place secure. You have good eyesight, and we'll need you to keep a careful eye on the cameras and keep listening to that radio in case some news gets broadcast. I know you are a fantastic shot, but that's another reason you must stay here.

Grandma, Paul, and Sue will need your help if the soldiers do come here."

Turning his attention to the group, Brad set up a plan. "We will break up into three groups. Steve, you take Jules and Tasha and head up to the old Faulkner place. George, you take Harold and Cassie and go to the Smiths'. Darren and Tonja, you will come with me. We will check out Bill Thompson's old farm.

"Stay together with your group. Try to stay away from the roadways. If you run into any soldiers, just stay out of sight. Let them leave before you continue.

"We don't want any loud noise or gunfire to cause the soldiers to come this direction. We are looking for food and weaponry. Not a fight.

"We will all meet back here by 10:00 p.m. It is 7:32 right now. A couple hours should give us all plenty of time to get to those places, scrounge a bit, and make it back here. Any questions?"

George asked, "Why did you separate us like that?"

"If you don't have your spouse to think about, you will respond better in an emergency. You can have faith your spouse is okay in another place. Is everyone ready?"

"You might want to go by my place before splitting up," Paul said. "At the far end of my barn, there is a ladder leaning up against the wall. Move it to the left, and look down. You will see a small hook in one of the floorboards. Push the hook straight back toward the wall. One of the boards will pop up. Under that board you will see a rope-and-pulley system I rigged into the wall. It's under and behind the boards. Pull the rope.

"Above and to the left there is a small section of false flooring on the loft rafters. It will reveal itself. Move the ladder over to it.

"This contains my stash of weaponry. Besides guns and ammo, there are two very nice, brand spanking new crossbows. Sorry, I don't have one for each group, but two silent armaments should help a little bit.

"I wish I was going with you guys, but I know my turn is coming, and when it does, I will make it count."

The band left the bunker and went to Paul's home.

First they checked out the house. In the basement they saw the bloodstains where Paul's wife and child had been killed, but there were no bodies.

Tasha thought, *I wonder what they did with the bodies.*

The band went to the barn to check out the stash Paul had told them about. They retrieved the weapons and ammo.

George stated to Harold, "I don't know the first thing about crossbows."

Harold stated, "I don't either. Maybe Brad and Steve's groups should take them. We'll take that .300 Winchester Mag and some ammo."

"That sounds good to me. I haven't done much shooting these last few years," responded George.

Feeling the need to remind them she was there and a part of their group, Cassie piped in, "I'm just fine with this." She raised the .223 she had carried with her from the bunker.

"Okay. Our group is fine. We are going to head over to the Smiths'. Stay safe. We'll meet you back at the bunker at ten," declared George to the other two groups as they started walking away from them.

Jules confessed, "I've never shot a crossbow before either, Dad."

Tasha stated matter-of-factly, "I have, and I'm pretty good with it."

Steve passed her the crossbow and arrows. Jules and Steve each grabbed some guns and ammo. They said their good-byes to Brad's group and set out toward the Faulkners'.

Brad said to his group, "Who wants the crossbow?"

The End Is Not Yet

Darren smiled, "I'll take it."

"Okay, but we'd better get going," Brad said. "Bill Thompson's is a little farther than the rest, so we'll have to hustle."

They were just about to reach the far side of the field they were cutting across when they heard some brush snap in the woods ahead of them.

"Get down," urged Brad. They all stooped as low as they could. "See that large tree over there?"

Looking to their right, they saw a huge-trunked tree that stood about ten feet away from the rest of the woods. They crept over to it until they were hidden by it.

They tried to see what had caused the noise, but the area was strangely quiet.

Then Tonja caught a glimpse of something that moved behind an old, downed log. Whatever it was, it was wearing a stocking cap. She gestured at Brad and pointed at the log.

Brad motioned for Darren to go around behind the person. Tonja was to keep her rifle sighted on that spot.

Crawling into the woods, Brad managed to get alongside the log.

Darren crept up from behind the area and made a noise to draw the person's attention. The person jumped up, turned away from the noise, and ran straight into Brad.

From the size of the person, Brad thought he was fighting with a child, so he held the person until he or she stopped struggling.

"What have we here?" said Brad. He pulled the stocking cap from the head of the child. To his amazement, it wasn't a child at all. It was a very young lady. Her big brown eyes showed nothing but terror as she stared at him.

"Please don't kill me. Please...please don't kill me." Her body went limp, and she collapsed in Brad's arms.

"It looks as if it's been a while since she's had something to eat," surmised Tonja.

Brad agreed with Tonja. "Yeah, I guess we won't be going over to Bill Thompson's. Let's get her back to the bunker."

***

George, Harold, and Cassie arrived at the Smiths'. All seemed quiet, so they started to scrounge for food.

Cassie looked in the cupboards. "That's odd."

"What's odd?" asked George.

"The cupboards. They still have food in them. A lot of food right, in plain sight. It's as if the soldiers and state police haven't been here yet," responded Cassie.

"Why is that odd?" asked Harold. "Let's take it and get out of here."

"Maybe that's exactly what they want us to do. They have already been to other homes in the area. Why would they leave this one alone and leave all this food here? Is it a trap? Dare we even touch these cans?" Cassie asked.

George told them to stand way back. He tossed an old shoe he found lying on the floor toward one end of the shelves. A couple cans fell over, but nothing happened. "It's not a booby trap."

Moving closer again to the cupboards, they each took a can from the shelf. Looking very closely at the can, Cassie saw a small hole in the side of it. She showed the hole to George. George and Harold inspected the cans they had picked up and saw the same thing.

Harold stated, "So it *is* a booby trap. Designed to kill us and anyone we try to feed it to. I would say they put poison in these cans."

"Good eye, Cassie," said George. "If you had not caught that, we could have killed our entire families. We'll have to inspect what we gather more carefully and let the others know to do the same." George paused for a moment to think. "The Smiths had a wine cellar. I remember them bringing some wine in from outside when I was here visiting. Let's see if we can find it."

They found an outside entrance to a cellar. The

latch was broken, and the door was ajar. The cellar was empty.

George stated, "I've got a feeling this is not the cellar we are looking for. Mr. Smith took pride in his wine collection and would not have kept it in a normal food cellar. Let's look a little more."

While searching around the garage, Cassie again noticed something was different than it should be. "Hey, guys, come here. Look at this garage. If you are looking at the inside, the wall goes about two feet beyond that side window to the back wall. If you look at it from the outside, the wall extends about four and a half feet past the side window to the back wall. There must be a false wall inside. Let's take a look."

It was true. There had to be some kind of room behind that wall.

They eventually found a loose board by the left window. After they pulled on it, a three-board panel on the back wall opened up.

There was a set of stairs behind it that led to a lower level under the garage. The stairs had walls on both sides. The left wall was the outside wall, and the right wall was to block up the inside room. This was to make the inside cellar more of a solid room to keep the wine cooler. It also made this a safe room in case of a tornado or some other short-term emergency.

"This must be it. Light some candles, and we'll

take a look," said George.

George led the way down the stairs. Harold followed, and Cassie brought up the rear, with her weapon ready. As they reached the bottom of the stairs and turned to the right, their eyes widened. What they saw sent chills up their spines, and they froze. They walked right into weapons staring them in the face. The rifle was snatched from Cassie's hands as if she had no hold of it at all.

Then they realized who their opponents were. Tabler and Rosie Smith and their children were held up in their wine cellar.

Mr. Smith demanded very angrily, "Hands in the air! Are you with the government?"

Tabler Smith, who was usually a decisive and outspoken person, had been caught off guard by everything happening in his homeland. He had frequently vented to his wife, Rosie, about how the government would be the downfall of this nation. He had said it, but he had always hoped he was wrong. He sure wasn't ready for it to happen now.

With everything happening so suddenly, it had left him doubting himself and his convictions. He had been wondering what he had missed. What had made him think he had so much more time to prepare? If he was wrong about when this was going to happen, what else was he wrong about?

Astonished by the question, George retorted, "Of course I'm not with the government. How long have you known me, Tabler? Have I ever given you cause to think I would do anything except love our country and the people in it?"

Tabler responded, "No, you haven't, but with what is happening now, I don't know who to trust anymore."

"You have to trust your instincts and the people you've known for so many years before this all started," stated George.

Things went silent, so Harold thought he would try for a bit of pity from his captors. "Can everyone relax now, before someone gets shot...like me?" said Harold. "I'd rather help heal a bullet wound than get one." He started to lower his arms.

Tabler didn't stop him. Sensing everything was really okay, Tabler Smith ordered his family to lower their weapons.

He admitted, "We are close to being out of food, but we've been hearing noises outside every day, so we've been trying to stay put. We didn't want to go outside until we knew it would be safe, or until we absolutely had to go out.

"We weren't really ready for this, you know. Who could be?"

George asked if they had left a lot of food in their cupboards in the house.

Rosie Smith said, "We left some we weren't able to get to, but I wouldn't call it a lot. Why?"

The End Is Not Yet

George told them about the food in the cupboards and what they had found.

"They probably thought we were still around, but couldn't find us, so they set a trap. By the way, how did you find us?" asked Tabler.

"Some of our women are right smart puzzle solvers," stated Harold, and he motioned toward Cassie.

"George, maybe we should take them back with us?" suggested Cassie.

"Well, we do still have room, and by the size of this room, I'll bet you guys are either sitting up to sleep, or rotating sleeping hours. There isn't much room in here. Why don't you pack up what you can, and come with us?" suggested George.

"There are seven of us. Are you sure you have room for that many? Like I said before, we don't have much food left," admitted Tabler.

"There's plenty of room, and as for food, we'll make it work. You can help us scrounge for more food on the way back," said George.

***

Steve asked, mostly to himself, "What do we do now?"

They had gotten to the Faulkners' just ahead of a band of soldiers that came there to scrounge. They hid behind some old crates stacked under the stairs in the basement. They listened while, above them, things were thrown about. They heard more soldiers arrive. They couldn't tell what the soldiers above them were saying, but there were two soldiers standing outside by the basement window, and they could hear them very well.

"They say this thing might last longer than we first thought," declared the first soldier. "We need to find these renegades and do away with them. I heard more got away than were figured on. They are causing all kinds of problems around Washington, DC. They even found a way into the Capitol and took some of the president's food."

"It serves him right. He's no good. He can't be trusted. He will probably have us killed if we can't show we have killed our quota of renegades," said the second soldier.

"Are you saying you would like to defect and help those renegades?" asked the first soldier.

"Well, it seems to me they care about each other. They help each other. The side we are fighting for is every man for himself. We'll be killed in the end. You mark my words," declared the second soldier.

"You won't have to wait for the end." With those words, the first soldier raised his rifle and shot his fellow soldier.

Steve, Jules, and Tasha shivered when they saw this, but they were able to remain quiet.

The End Is Not Yet

Steve whispered, "We need to find a way out of this basement. They will more than likely check down here for supplies before they leave."

The soldiers in the house ran outside to see what the gunfire was about.

"He was going to defect and help those stinkin' renegades," said the first soldier. "He was a traitor. I stopped him."

Another soldier yelled, "That was Teaser. He wouldn't have defected. He was a soldier through and through. He knew if he did defect, his family would be in danger. They would be imprisoned and killed the same as any other renegade. He would never have put their lives in danger like that."

Things got heated outside, and the arguing continued.

"This is our chance," said Steve. "Let's sneak upstairs and try to get out the back while their attention is on this. They aren't thinking about anyone else being around right now. Go! Go!"

They got outside but had to crawl across a field to avoid being seen. When they reached the other side, they heard another rifle shot.

The soldier who was a friend of Teaser lay dead beside his buddy. They heard the first soldier yell in triumph, "We just added two more to our quota, and their families!" He continued to laugh.

A soldier came around the end of the house. It

appeared that he had seen the group, so being sharp and quick, Tasha raised the crossbow, took careful aim, and shot him in the mouth just as he was about to shout an alert to the others. He never had the chance to take a breath, much less say a word. It happened swiftly and silently, and there the dead soldier lay.

Soldiers continued to argue beside the two dead soldiers on the lawn. None of the soldiers realized what had just happened.

***

It was now past the time Steve, Tasha, and Jules were supposed to be back at the bunker. Brad and Debbie were beginning to wonder what had become of them. Brad tried to reassure Debbie. "I told them if soldiers were around, to stay hidden until they left," said Brad. "They are probably doing just that. Waiting it out. Don't worry. We'll give them a little more time then we'll go look for them."

While keeping his eyes off the monitors, Troy announced, "Someone's coming. It's Dad, Jules, and Aunt Tasha. They seem to be okay. No one is following them."

Arriving safely inside the bunker, Steve immediately reported what had happened and the conversations they had overheard. "Something is really wrong," he said. "Even the soldiers don't trust each other. To just shoot someone as if he was a rabid dog? What is this world coming to? That soldier seemed to have a soft spot in his heart for his fellow humans, and it got him killed."

Debbie asked, "No one stepped in and tried to stop it?"

Tasha responded, "They either believed in what was happening, or they were afraid they'd be killed too."

The family and friends listened in disbelief to the stories about the cruelty that was happening in their homeland.

After much thought, Tasha asked, "How will we be able to tell who is on our side? It appears that even some in uniform are on our side. There might be more people in uniform *not* doing this because they believe in it. They could be forced to serve. I don't want to start distrusting everyone. There just have to be more good people out there."

Debbie stated, "I have started reading the Bible more since this all began. I think this passage fits what is happening now."

Debbie opened the Bible, found the passage in 2 Timothy, and read:

But know this, that in the last days perilous times will come. For men will be lovers of themselves, lovers of money, boasters, proud, blasphemers, disobedient to parents, unthankful, unholy, unloving, unforgiving, slanderers, without self-control, brutal, despisers of good, traitors, headstrong, haughty, lovers of pleasure rather than lovers of God, having a form of godliness but denying its power. And from such people turn away!

Debbie stopped to add her own thoughts. "The Bible forewarned us this would happen. We will just have to watch and listen to how a person portrays himself or herself, and make our best judgments from that. It will get a lot worse before it gets better."

"Who are our guests?" asked Jules.

George had met Tabler while he was doing side jobs as a mechanic on farm equipment to earn extra money. He needed the cash when Tasha was going through cancer treatments. Realizing that the rest of the family did not know the Smiths, George introduced Tabler and Rosie to the family.

From there, Tabler took the opportunity to continue the introductions. "These are Karen and Josie, our teen and almost-teen wonders. We *wonder* if they will ever make it to adulthood."

This brought laughter from the group as the two girls started to blush.

"This little gal is Candice. She should fit right in with your Paisley and Mary.

"And then we have Thomas. He has the wits of the family. He likes to tinker with things, even as young as he is. I'm sure he will try to entice your Marty into designing new vehicles, machinery, and, maybe even some robots with those Legos.

"This fine young man is Justin, my brother. He just turned twenty-one. We were going to celebrate his birthday next weekend with the folks. He was visiting when the soldiers came. We have no idea what has happened to our parents or our younger brother Clark."

Marty took Thomas to the children's area, where they could play and get to know each other better. They played with the Gameboys for a short time. They played with trucks, and tried their hand at pretending to be Batman and the Joker.

They had just started to build a forest with the Legos when Thomas decided to tell Marty a joke.

"Hey, Marty, wanna hear a joke?"

"Sure, Thomas, what is it?" asked Marty.

"Well, you have to close your eyes." Thomas waved his hands back and forth. He was close to the sides of Marty's cheeks but wasn't touching them. "Can you feel the breeze?" said Thomas.

"Yup!" replied Marty. "The breeze feels nice."

"Now imagine you are running through the woods. You are running faster and faster. Keep your eyes closed. Can you still feel the breeze?" Thomas continued to wave his hands faster and faster past Marty's cheeks. "Can you imagine the trees going by as you are running past them?"

"Oh, yes. This is so cool!" remarked Marty.

Thomas used the palm of his hand to slap Marty on the forehead.

Shocked, Marty opened his eyes and asked, "What'd ya do that for?"

"You're not supposed to run through the woods with your eyes closed. You'll run into a tree!" Thomas started laughing so hard he fell to the floor and started rolling around.

After the shock wore off, Marty realized how funny the joke really was. He joined Thomas in the laughter.

Mary started crying and ran to Cassie, who was in the kitchen area. "Mommy, Thomas is being mean to Marty. He said it was a joke, but it wasn't. He just wanted to be mean to him."

Cassie said, "Mary, you must have misunderstood. Maybe you should tell me what happened."

Mary proceeded to tell her mom the joke. "Now close your eyes." Cassie closed her eyes as instructed. Mary started waving her arms past her mom's face. Mary told her mom to imagine she was running through the woods. Then, without warning, Mary doubled up her fist and punched her mom square on the nose. Cassie's eyes flew open.

The End Is Not Yet

Cassie asked Mary, "Why'd you hit me?"

Seeing the startled look on her mom's face, Mary blurted, "You're not a'post to have your eyes closed."

Cassie grabbed her daughter and started to tickle her. Soon everyone was laughing, just as much from the joke as from Mary's version of it.

Darren, who had been in the surveillance room, entered the kitchen area. "What's everyone laughing about?" he said.

Marty turned to his dad. "Let me tell you a joke."

Chapter 4

A Thief Among Us

Debbie and Rosie were talking about what they should prepare for the group for supper.

"Maybe everyone would like some of that Beef Stroganoff we have in the cans," suggested Rosie.

"Okay. They might enjoy a change from the usual things we've been making. It's stashed in the back of the food storage. I'll go dig it out," offered Debbie.

As Debbie was moving some of the cases of food around to get to the Beef Stroganoff, she noticed some empty cans hidden behind the boxes. The empty cans had once contained some ready-made foods. That food had been set aside for scrounging groups. On missions they could easily carry them, open the cans, and eat the contents without having to cook anything. There were also some empty candy bar wrappers.

Debbie thought this was strange. She couldn't think of anyone in the group selfish enough to steal food when so many people's lives depended on it.

She decided to keep this to herself for now. She would keep an eye on things until she knew who was stealing.

***

Karen and Josie Smith were typical teenage girls. They liked playing with each other's hair, experimenting with makeup, and teasing the boys.

In the short time they had been there, Josie had already acquired a liking for Troy. She realized that Madelyn had a crush on Troy too. This made them rivals for his attention, but to them that just made the games more fun. They were always trying to one-up each other, hoping that Troy would notice. Karen, however, secretly had a crush on Earl.

The girls enjoyed being around Madelyn. She was older but seemed to fit right in with them.

Since Karen and Josie had arrived, Madelyn was even more relaxed in her surroundings. She would laugh and joke with them. The three seemed inseparable. They had even gained the nickname "the three musketeers." Sometimes people wondered why it wasn't "the three stooges."

However, there were still times that Madelyn

would go off by herself in another bunker. She didn't really look at herself as part of the group. Inside, she felt her sins were beyond her. She felt she could never be forgiven for the secrets she had to keep.

Karen walked down the hallway to the restroom. She had just about closed the door when a hand grabbed the edge of it. She stopped closing the door and allowed it to be opened. She thought someone just needed to grab something quickly out of the room before she closed the door.

"What's up?" Karen asked. "Oh, it's you. Did you want something before I use the facilities?"

Earl stood in the doorway. As she allowed the door to open back up, he slid inside the room. He closed the door behind him. "I've been noticing how much you've been looking at me. It makes me feel real warm inside to know you have feelings for me."

He moved closer to her. He placed his hand on her waist and started to slide his arm around to her back. "You know, we could consummate our love for each other," he said, "and then we would be married. No one would have to know." With his other hand he touched her breast. He pulled her closer and was about to kiss her.

Karen raised her knee and caught him right in the crotch. She shoved him back at the same time.

She glared at him. "You ever do something like

that again, and you'll be sorry. I used to like you, but now I just think you're puke." She pretended to gag. She boldly walked past him and left the restroom. By now she had forgotten that she had to relieve herself.

After that, Karen totally ignored Earl. She felt rather proud of the way she had handled the situation.

Karen and Josie noticed that Madelyn's times of seclusion would happen not too long after Madelyn would say or do something her brother didn't like.

Earl would lean over and whisper something to her, and Madelyn would get very quiet. Earl would sit with a silly smirk on his face, as if he was the king of the world, and soon Madelyn would be off by herself.

One day Josie and Karen decided they wanted to know exactly why Madelyn would get into these moods and hide. They decided to follow her. When they found her in one of the storage bunkers, she was crying.

Josie asked her, "Why are you crying? We were having so much fun. What is it that Earl says to you that upsets you so?"

With a face full of tears, Madelyn responded meekly, "I can't tell you."

"Sure you can," urged Karen. "It can't be all that bad. It looks as if he has been bullying you. If you let him, he'll keep treating you like this. You need to stand up to him."

"You don't understand. I really can't tell you. He will hurt anyone I talk to about it. He told me he would hurt our father if I told him. I didn't believe him. I told my father...and...Earl killed him." Madelyn didn't want to say anything else.

"What? Your mother told everyone that the soldiers killed your dad," Josie said.

"No. My mother told everyone *Earl* said the soldiers killed our dad.

"I was there. I saw Earl do it. He told me if I told Mom, he would kill her too. That's when we met Mom coming back from the store. He told her a lie. I knew if I said anything, he would kill both of us, so I kept quiet.

"I had to keep it a secret from then on. I couldn't do anything to help anyone," said Madelyn remorsefully.

Speaking almost in a whisper, Karen asked, "What did Earl do that was so terrible, he was willing to kill your father?"

Madelyn repeated, "I can't tell you. He will kill you too. I don't want to be responsible for more deaths."

Karen confided in her friend. "I know what Earl can be like. I was going to use the restroom one night, and he followed me. He tried to get sexual with me. I had to fight him off. He's a real puke. You shouldn't even concern yourself with him. If he killed your father, he must have hit him when he wasn't looking. Earl doesn't have much backbone."

Josie assured Madelyn, "You can tell us. There are some good people who live in this bunker. They won't let him do anything to you, your mother, or us. He needs to be stopped from his evil ways, and only you can stop him. Please tell us, and let us help you. The adults will know how to handle him."

Not sure if she should really tell them her secret or not, Madelyn started to cry again. She was feeling so torn over everything.

She finally decided it was time to trust someone else. She had a hard time choosing how to say what she was about to disclose to her two young friends.

As if all the sorrow inside her could not be held back any longer, she blurted out, "He does things to me no brother should do to his sister. He touches me where he is not supposed to. He doesn't let me see what, but he puts something inside me between my legs, and sometimes up my butt. It hurts. I pretend like I'm not there."

The girls' eyes filled with tears, for the pain, they could see, was destroying their friend. Josie said, "We'll tell our mom. She'll know what to do, so no one gets hurt. Come with us, so he can't catch you in here by yourself."

While the three girls were having their

conversation in the storage bunker, Earl was taking sick.

Harold checked him over and hoped it wasn't a virus or something contagious that could make the entire group ill.

Talking to Sue, he was mystified. "It appears Earl might have food poisoning; but if it was food poisoning, why is he the only one who's sick?"

The illness was taking Earl fast. Whatever poison was in his system, it was not going to let him survive. He was sweating and convulsing in pain. Soon he succumbed to the poison, and it was all over. Harold never had the chance to really help him.

Harold reported to the group, "I have been thinking that food poisoning is what made Earl sick, but we all eat the same things every meal. None of us ever eats anything special. No one else is sick."

Debbie revealed to the group what she had found when she went into the food storage bunker. "We need to take a closer look at those empty cans, and the rest of our food. Maybe we missed some contaminated cans."

They took a good look at some of the cans that had been emptied by the food thief. Sure enough, one of the cans of spaghetti had a little piece of rubberized sealant on the side of it. They checked the entire food supply again. They found what used to be a six-pack of spaghetti. Each can had a tiny piece of sealant on the side.

Josie and Karen took Madelyn back to the storage bunker where they had had their talk. The two girls told their friend they would never tell anyone what they knew about Earl. He was gone now, and telling the rest would only upset Esther needlessly. It would be their secret. Madelyn wouldn't have to feel bad anymore. Earl would never be able to hurt her or anyone else again.

Chapter 5

The Escapee

After examining Paul's wound, Harold stated, "It looks real good. How do you feel?"

Paul stretched. "I feel as if I could go out on the next scavenger hunt." He continued talking as he exited the medical storage room. "I'm ready to bury my family and say my good-byes."

Tasha spoke hesitantly. "We looked for them when we went to your home for the guns. The bodies were not there. We wanted to tell you sooner, but you were hurt. There was nothing that could be done at that point, so we decided it was best to wait." Tasha lowered her eyes and wondered if they had made the right decision.

Paul turned away to hide the tears welling in his eyes. After a few short moments, he wiped his eyes and turned back to Tasha. He realized her need for acceptance for their actions and responded in a barely audible voice. "I understand. That was very kind of you." He then turned and retreated to his sleeping area to be alone.

Debbie questioned, "I wonder what they wanted the bodies for."

***

When the young lady finally awoke, she was screaming. "Don't kill me. Please, please, please don't kill me. I don't want to be crispies. Please don't kill me."

Sue, thinking the girl must still be delirious, moved to her side, but not so fast as to frighten her. Speaking softly, Sue tried to soothe her fears. "No one's going to hurt you. You are safe here with us."

She put an arm loosely around the girl. Finally the girl calmed down a little, realizing that no one was moving toward her to do her any harm. She turned into Sue's arms and allowed Sue to hold her quietly. She remained that way for an hour.

Sue asked her, "Would you mind telling me your name?"

The young girl whispered in Sue's ear, "I'm Diti." It was as though Diti wasn't sure whom she could trust. She didn't want to give out too much information about herself just yet.

Sue asked her, "Would you like something to drink and eat?"

Diti accepted the drink but looked strangely at the food. It was as if she was inspecting it before taking a bite. Maybe she heard about the contaminated food the soldiers had left at the Smiths'. She continued to inspect each bite before putting it in her mouth. Once she put it in her mouth, she would move it around, as if checking the texture and flavor, before swallowing. It was as if she knew something the others didn't. It could have been just an overactive imagination, but somehow that did not seem to be the case. She obviously did not trust what they were trying to feed her, but she was so hungry and had no choice but to eat it.

"What could be causing her to act like this? If it were me, I'd be downing that, and asking for more before someone took it away!" said Jules.

Darren scoffed. "If it were you, you'd eat it now and ask if anyone else wanted some when you were on the last bite!"

Harold asked Sue to give the young girl a sedative to help her rest. The girl resisted, but she accepted it cautiously from Sue.

Jules mumbled, "She sure is pretty. I wonder who she is."

No one had seen her around before.

"She can't be more than twenty or twenty-one," Tonja guessed. "I wonder where her family is. If they are alive, I'm sure they're wondering where she is."

After a few hours, the young girl awakened. She was a little calmer than before. She realized that if these people wanted to kill or defile her, they would have done so already.

No one realized she was awake until she spoke. "Are my father, brothers, and little sisters here?"

Diti had not seen her family, but she hoped they were safe there too. Her hopes were soon crushed.

"No. Everyone here is who you see. There is no one else," stated Jules in the kindest voice he could manage. "I'm Jules. What is your name?"

"I'm Diti. My real name is Aphrodite, but I don't like it."

Laughing lightly, Jules confessed, "My real name is Julius, as in Caesar. I don't like it either. Maybe our folks were making bad jokes."

Jules asked, "Where are you from? Why were you out there alone?"

The first impression of Diti was a giddy, unstable teenager. In reality, she was a lot older than her years. She had an inner strength that seemed to show up just when she needed it most. This became evident as she revealed the story of what happened to her and her family.

"I'm from La Crosse. My family and I were taken by the police. We couldn't understand why. We had done as the president commanded. We didn't hold anything back. They took us to an encampment and separated us. I haven't seen my father or my two older brothers since then.

"My older brothers had been away at college. They came home when this all started. They were hoping to be able to help us. Instead they were taken along with us to the encampment. They should have stayed away."

The emotional hurt that drained her body as she continued was evident. "My mom, my two younger sisters, and I were taken to a separate complex. It looked like a hospital. We had no idea what they had planned to do with us. We thought they might use us for experiments, but I found out it was much worse than that. The morning after they captured us, they came and took my two little sisters." She started to cry uncontrollably.

Jules put his arm around her lightly, so as not to rekindle her earlier fears. "Diti, maybe you should just forget about it."

Before he could finish, Diti blurted, "How can I forget about such a horrible thing that happened to my family?"

"I didn't mean forget about it. I meant maybe you should forget about *telling* us about it for now. It will never be easier to talk about, but maybe with a little more rest..."

Diti stated, "I have no time to rest. I have to tell

you. Maybe you can help my family and the others. If there is anyone left to help.

"Like I said, I don't know what they did with my older brothers and my father. When I was escaping, I saw a large cattle pen that had been made into a cage. It had a lot of men in it. I couldn't see everyone in it, though. They had them so crammed into it, they couldn't bend over. It looked like they'd have to sleep standing up. There must have been two hundred men held up in a pen meant for fifty cows."

Jules asked, "Where is your mom? Do you know where they took your little sisters?"

"Two soldiers came to get my mom and me. One soldier grabbed my mom. He was so strong. He practically carried my mom out the door instead of letting her walk on her own two feet. The other one grabbed me. My mom and I were struggling all the way down the hallway.

"I was falling farther and farther behind the other soldier and my mom. The soldier I was fighting with finally decided it might be easier to just carry me too. So when he took me from behind and started to raise me up, I kicked as hard as I could backward. The heel of my shoe landed right where it was supposed to. He dropped me like a hot potato and grabbed his groin. I was able to get away.

"I ran down the hallway and around a corner. I

ran into a room on the side. It looked like some type of kitchen. Some oversized pots were on a stove. A door went out the other side of the room, but, not knowing where that room led, I decided to find a hiding place in this room. I knew I didn't have much time. That soldier would be right behind me.

"There was one exceptionally large, empty vat on top of the stove, with a lid sitting along side it. I decided I might just be able to fit in it. I pushed the other door so it would be ajar. Then I climbed up on the stove and squeezed into that pot. I was just shutting the lid over me when I heard the hall door open. I prayed that he had not seen me.

"He saw the door to the next room was open and continued through it. When I thought I had waited long enough that he wouldn't be coming back, I got out of the pot.

"I crept down the hallway and looked for a way out. I looked in this one room. Some little girls were strapped in the beds. They appeared to be sedated. They were naked, and their legs were spread open. Their...their...vaginal areas and nipples had been removed. Even their earlobes had been cut off. It looked as though some kind of medicine had been applied to stop the bleeding.

"On a table close to the beds were two trays. One tray contained the vaginal lips. On the other tray I saw the earlobes and nipples. They were soaking in some kind of solution.

The End Is Not Yet

"I didn't understand what was happening. I kept asking myself why they would be torturing these little girls in such a way. What could they have done to deserve this? Why would they allow them to live after this? Why not just kill them and get it over with?

"I couldn't help them. They couldn't walk. They were sleeping. I couldn't carry them. I had to leave them. I wished I were fifteen people at that moment, instead of just me. I had to continue on. You understand, don't you?"

Jules nodded, but he was so shocked by what he was hearing he couldn't say anything.

Diti continued, "I snooped around a bit more, trying to find my way out. I was hoping to find a way to help these people escape. I went into the lower basement area. I had to hide again. Some soldiers were bringing in something wrapped in plastic.

"I overheard them talking. One was saying he wanted some of those deep-fried crispies. The other one told him he would never be able to afford them. He told him that the crispies were to be saved for the president and his influential guests. He said the crispies were shipped straight to the White House from the encampments all over the country. Everyone else was left with hamburger. He made me want to vomit when he said even that tasted sweet. The other soldier said they get a good price for the crispies. He said the crispies from the youngsters were crispy on the outside and creamy on the inside so they brought a higher price than the old fogies. He said the ones from the old fogies are supposed to be just like eating those deep-fried pigskins. They talked about how they would eat either one. There is supposed to be such a market out there that they couldn't understand why the price had to remain so high.

"It made me wonder what they were talking about, but then they unwrapped what they had carried in the plastic. It was a female carcass that had been quartered. The vaginal area had been removed as had happened to the little girls, but the entire breast had been removed on this woman.

"They hung the quarters on the hooks above the table, and set the woman's head on the table. They dropped the plastic into a barrel at the far end of the table, and left.

"After waiting to make sure they were gone, I climbed out of my hiding place. As I passed the end of the table to leave the room, an uneasy feeling came over me. I had to look back at the table. I became so violently ill from what I saw, I had to rush to the other end of the table and vomit in the barrel."

Choking back the need to vomit again, Diti cried out, "It was my mother. They killed my mother." Almost inaudibly, she continued, choking on her words. "They killed her and were preparing to make her into food."

After a few moments of weeping, Diti continued, "I couldn't just leave her, and I couldn't carry her, so I took her head. I carried her as gently as I could. I was determined she would have some kind of burial. She was such a wonderful mother. She deserved at least that.

"I stopped snooping around. I decided to find my way out of there. I figured that if I got away, I could bring back some help for my father, brothers, and maybe my two little sisters. But I really don't have much hope that they're alive."

Gasps and gagging came from the entire group as they listened to what this young girl was saying.

Brad stated, "We will have to go out on more excursions. We will need to scavenge for more ammo and food. But I for one won't be able to stay here and do nothing while those people suffer."

The rest chimed in that they were ready to do whatever was necessary.

"The government will not win this battle." Brad was adamant about that.

Paul's shoulders sunk. "Now I know why they took the bodies. Let's get going. I'm ready to take out as many of those bastards as I can! First we will need to go to my place again. I have a lot of food stashed. Its location was too complicated for me to tell you where it was before, but now I can show you.

"We should take the truck and the ATV. It will make the hauling go faster. What we can't fit in the vehicles, we can hand-carry. I warn you, there is a lot."

Brad suggested, "We should wait until tomorrow, especially if there is as much as you say. It will take time to haul it, and time to put it all away when we get it here.

"We can make our plans for the mission, and get a good night's sleep, before we go out again."

It was agreed by all that that sounded like the best thing to do.

Everyone went to bed early that night. No one really wanted to socialize after what they had just heard from Diti.

***

The next morning, plans were made to get the supplies from Paul's farm. They also made the plans for the next day, when they would go out on the rescue mission.

Paul was right about having a lot of supplies. When they were done hauling, they realized the one bunker for storage was totally full. There was enough food to feed a lot of people for a long time. There were also plenty of seeds for planting when they could finally live safely aboveground again.

The End Is Not Yet

Now they needed to turn their efforts toward finding more ammo and weapons.

The day was pretty well used up. As planned, they would settle in and rest before heading out on their rescue mission. They were all feeling a bit antsy to get going on their rescue mission, but they knew their own safety, and the safety of the others in the bunker, had to come first. They needed to relax their minds, and for the family, that meant a game was in order. Tasha asked, "Who's up for a game of Scrabble? Maybe it will help us relax a bit."

George, Steve, Tonja, and Cassie agreed that was a great idea. George went first. He laid down BRRR and started to count the points.

Tasha smirked. "What are you doing? I don't think that's allowed as a word."

"Yes it is," George argued. "I used it on the video game version, and the system allowed it. So there!"

Next to play was Steve. He played the word BENZYLS and was able to take a double word score for it.

Tasha sighed. "I can just see what this game is going to be like."

They all laughed.

Debbie, who was usually pretty understanding, but was cautious and almost too skeptical at times, took Brad off to the side of the room. "I'm not sure I believe our little friend over there," Debbie said.

"She said she carried her mother's head. She never said she put it in anything. That leads me to believe she just plain carried it. It would have had to get against her clothes, but there aren't any bloodstains. I wonder how she managed that.

"Is it possible she is a spy sent here to find our location for the government? We are getting to be quite a large group. There are over thirty of us now. We are a thorn in the local soldiers' sides. Her story is pretty outrageous, don't you think?"

Brad responded, "It doesn't matter what I really think. We can't take the chance of endangering all these people. Let's play it by ear while we gather the necessary weaponry and ammo. I'll warn everyone to use extra caution outside."

Jules had gone to the water pump to get a drink of water, and happened to overhear Brad and Debbie's conversation. He told Darren what he had heard. He asked Darren, "Do you think it's possible?"

Darren suggested, "Let's ask her. We'll hear what she has to say, and then decide what to do."

Jules and Darren went straight to Diti. They talked to her very quietly, so as not to arouse any unwarranted suspicions.

Jules decided to ask her straight out. "How did you get past all those soldiers between here and there?"

The End Is Not Yet

Diti responded, "I just kept quiet and only moved when no one was around. It took a long time. I thought I had had it when you guys caught me."

Darren asked, "Some have been wondering how you were able to avoid getting your clothes dirty on such a trip."

"When I realized how bad my clothes had gotten, I decided to borrow some different clothes from a house that I stopped at just before you caught me. I buried my mom, and then realized how much of her blood I had gotten on me. I hated to wash it off. It was all I had left of my family. Why are you asking me all this? Don't you believe me?" inquired Diti.

"There are a lot of people here we feel a responsibility to. We just have to be sure of who we put our trust in," admitted Darren.

Jules stated, "I believe you, but you have to admit, your story does sound pretty far-fetched. Can you prove what you say is true?"

Without a second thought, Diti stated, "I can take you to where I buried my mother, and show you what I did with the clothes I took off. It's not far from here. Will that help to prove this?"

"Let's go now, while it is dark," Darren suggested. "The rest are involved in their game. Just the three of us will go. We'll bring back the bloody clothes to show Grandpa and Grandma."

With the others involved in the game, the three of them were able to slip out without being noticed. Diti led Jules and Darren to the Smiths' home. In the backyard was a rose garden. Diti showed them where she had buried her mother's head among the rosebushes. She told the men what she had been thinking.

"She always loved flowers. I thought it was where she would want to be. I didn't think the owners would have minded if they knew the type of person my mom was."

Then she led them to a garbage can beside the back door of the house. She lifted the lid. There were her bloody clothes.

Jules stated, "I knew you were telling the truth."

As if hearing the entire story all over again, a realization and a feeling of disbelief came over him. "Then this means...the rest of the story was true too. Our government is harvesting us for food." Suddenly a feeling of nausea engulfed him. He ran to the corner of the house to hide his vomiting.

They returned to the bunker. They showed their grandpa and grandma the bloody clothes. The five agreed that the rest of the group would never be told of their excursion. They figured that the more doubt and mistrust could be kept away from the group, the better.

Diti had been through enough, but they all knew it was not over.

The End Is Not Yet

The five Scrabble players were still going at it.

"This game is turning into a Scrabble game for people with master's degrees," laughed Tonja, and she played the word *ZAXES*.

"Wait a minute," said Steve, "What on Earth is *ZAXES*?"

They all laughed, and the game went on.

Hearing the laughter and fun the others were having together upset Paul. He paced around the bunker for a while, deep in thought. He remembered all the fun times he had had with his wife and little boy. He had always prided himself on being able to take care of them and keep them safe.

Then this had happened, and there was nothing he could do to help them. He was so against violence that he had hidden his stash of weapons too far away to get to when he needed it.

He soon stated, "I'm kind of tired. I think I'll go lie down for a while." He retreated to his sleeping area.

Chapter 6

Vengeance Realized

The more Paul thought about it, the more he felt the only way he could ever live with himself was to avenge his family. The best way to do this was to take out as many soldiers and as much of their supplies as he could. This would ultimately help the rest of humankind. His family would live on in the thankful hearts and minds of those he helped.

Deep in his heart, he promised his wife and son this would happen.

Later that evening, Paul came back to the dining room. This time he had his coat on. He announced he was going to take a walk. He couldn't stand being cooped up right now. He needed the outdoors to help him clear his head.

"I'd like to go for a walk too," Justin said. "Would you care if I tag along, Paul? The rest are playing a game. I'm not that much into games, and I'm feelin' kinda bored. Besides, none of us should really be going out alone."

Not really wanting any company, but realizing the rest might think it strange if he insisted on going out alone, Paul responded, "I guess you can come, but I warn you, I may not be doing much talking."

"That's okay," said Justin. "I really just want some fresh air too."

They gathered some guns and ammo in case they ran into the enemy. They stepped outside. The night air was cool and crisp.

"This is refreshing," said Justin. "It's just the right temperature for a stroll, although it's not quite cool enough to wear a coat."

"You know, I wasn't just coming out for a stroll. You should probably go back to the bunker," advised Paul.

"I didn't really take you for the strolling type," replied Justin. "So what's really on your mind? You know they have probably taken and possibly even killed my parents and younger brother.

"We didn't have any bunker or hiding place to take refuge in. My parents thought that preparing for the worst was a waste of time and money. They never thought anything like this would happen, because we live in the United States.

"Point being, I'd like to get a hold of a few of those soldiers myself. Maybe get some information about where my family might be.

"My little brother is only seventeen. He hasn't done anything to deserve being taken or killed by those monsters."

Paul realized he might have a comrade-in-arms. "I was pondering taking a stroll back home. Maybe follow some tracks left by certain trucks, and see what I can find out."

Justin was just young enough, and physically fit enough, to feel as if he could conquer the world. He had been so talented at electronic combat games, he felt that he could save his family single-handedly.

"I'm with you all the way," declared Justin.

"We'll have to hustle. The others will soon realize we haven't just taken a walk. You up to it?" asked Paul.

"You lead. I'll be right behind you every step of the way," replied Justin. It was meant to be a joke, but it didn't really come out right, so Justin let the conversation drop.

They travelled through the woods at a pretty good clip, but they still maintained precautions so they wouldn't get caught.

When they arrived at Paul's home, Paul went down to the basement to check for evidence of where the soldiers might have taken the bodies of his wife and son. Tears came to his eyes again as he relived the horrible sight of seeing them killed.

Paul didn't find anything. Determined to find some clue, Paul and Justin scouted out the surrounding area. Based on footprints that weaved in and out of the woods along the edge of the road, it appeared as though some of the soldiers walked through the woods looking for people. Others stayed in the trucks and rode along the roadside. The tracks headed due south from Paul's farm.

Paul and Justin followed the signs for quite some time.

Justin, feeling a bit weary, suggested, "Maybe we should stop for a short rest. It's not like we are going to catch up to them. Didn't they come to your home a few days ago?"

"Okay, we'll take a short break," agreed Paul. Before long, however, he said, "There are a lot of farms in this area. They still could be searching them. After all, they would want to catch anyone who tried to return home. So they would probably return to some of the places they have already checked. Don't you think?"

As if in answer to his question, they heard trucks in the distance. They moved slowly in the direction of the noise. Three trucks were just pulling into a clearing. It looked as though they thought it was break time too. As they were getting close, Paul and Justin decided to separate to perform better surveillance of the situation.

"If either of us is taken, the other needs to agree not to try to help him. It would be more advantageous for the free one to head back to the bunker. He can let the rest know what happened. Agreed?" said Paul. He continued, "There are too many of them for the two of us to take them out, so we will only try to gather information. This is not a combat mission. Agreed?"

Justin heard Paul's tone of voice and knew it would be a waste of time to argue. He agreed to the plan. They separated, and each tried to get a little closer to the group of soldiers to hear their conversations and possibly gather some information. Paul watched as Justin went behind a log. A couple of soldiers walked up to the log and decided to sit on it for a smoke and a little conversation.

Justin lay as low as he could. He practically squeezed himself underneath the log to avoid being seen. He began to sweat from the fear that he might be captured. If he was taken captive, it would ruin everything. He would never be able to help his family. He would never see Tabler, Rosie, or the kids again. He spoke silently from his heart: "God, please help me."

One of the soldiers was about to swing his leg over the top of the log to straddle it. In so doing, he would be able to see Justin.

Paul made an intentional movement but tried to make it appear to Justin that it was an accident. The soldiers were alerted, and ran with their guns aimed directly at Paul. Paul allowed them to chase him right into their camp. Paul stopped and raised his arms as if to surrender.

Justin, watching all of this, started toward the soldiers. As he watched the soldiers gather around Paul, he noticed Paul had loosened his coat. As the soldiers drew closer, Paul opened his coat for them to see a hidden treasure.

Justin saw it at the same time he heard the blast. Paul had booby-trapped himself with ten grenades that he had found in the bunker ammo storage room and tied around his waist. Everything and everyone in that camp was in pieces.

There was nothing left for Justin to do except return to the bunker and tell the waiting group what had happened.

***

"Don't you go getting any fancy ideas, young man," ordered Tabler. "We will need every person we've got to make it through this. You included. So if you've got any notion of following in Paul's footsteps, you'd better get that right out of your head."

After much self-reflection, Justin countered, "I

don't have any notion to do anything like that, Tab. Not yet. I believe our family is still alive, and I want to be around when we find them. After that, I'll decide what I do."

Tabler pleaded with his brother. "Everyone thought Paul was handling the death of his family well. He thought about others' feelings. He talked fine. He acted fine. But to plan to commit murder and suicide is not fine.

"Those who commit suicide will never enter the kingdom of God. If any of us thought Paul was going to do something like that, we would have stopped him. At least we would have tried. In the end, he might have done this anyway, but now no one will ever know. He needed to give himself time to start thinking straight. He didn't do that.

"Think about it, Justin. We have only killed to protect ourselves and others. We have not deliberately gone out to kill anyone. Not even the soldiers. The Lord has helped our family survive so far. We weren't prepared for this, but the Lord saw to it that those who found us were good people.

"There are those who are saying that we are in the last days. If this really is going to be the end of *this* world, I don't think the Lord wants to start a new world with people who have vengeance in their hearts. If I make it there, I *really* want you there with me to help rebuild. What do ya say?"

"You know, Tab, I knew you and the family went

to church a lot, but I've never really heard you talk like this before."

Tabler, showing the softer side of himself and feeling the need to be open with his brother, responded, "The changes that are happening now would make anyone stop and think about what he truly believes in. I really do love the Lord and believe in him. I don't want to be left behind when he comes to take those who love him home."

After taking a moment to absorb what Tabler had just said, and thinking about the events of the night, Justin said, "Tab, I don't think Paul ever planned to come back to the bunker. That's why he didn't want anyone to go with him. He deliberately got caught to save me." Justin looked off to the side instead of at Tabler. "I'll think about what you said."

Chapter 7

Strangers in the Midst

The next morning, the entire bunker was up and buzzing earlier than usual. Everyone was well rested, and they would soon be well fed and ready to take on the soldiers and state police. It would be a long trek, but they were anxious to help the people in the encampment.

Looking down at the food she was preparing for breakfast, Debbie asked, "Will we have enough food and enough room if there are as many people as Diti says there are?"

"I guess we'll just have to work it out. We haven't run short of either yet," stated Brad.

Debbie, reflecting on everything that had happened since they went underground, stated, "That is true. Somehow there has always been enough of everything." *It's almost as if we are being watched over,* she thought.

The End Is Not Yet

Diti discussed the location of the encampment with Brad. Then she showed them the way. Jules and Brad were close at her side.

After traveling many miles on foot, they found a wooded area with enough brush and downed logs to hide the group. Brad called for everyone to take a rest. It had been hours since they had eaten, so this would be a good time for them to do that. Everyone was told to eat something cold. The smell of food cooking might alert nearby soldiers to their location.

After eating, Brad decided to scout ahead. He told the others to stay back and rest. He would come back and let them know what he found.

Feeling guilty about letting his grandpa go alone, Darren said, "Grandpa, I'd like to go with you."

"We don't know how far we have to go, or what's up ahead. You should try to rest while you can," suggested Brad.

"Then why don't you let me go, and you get some rest?" questioned Darren.

"I'd like to see what's up ahead for myself," Brad responded.

Darren decided to try a more joking approach to get Brad to let him go. "Hey, Grandpa, ever wonder why some people are called old farts? Because the stench is *slower* to dissipate. If I can't go instead of you, at least let me go with you."

After a short chuckle, Brad agreed. "Okay, you can go with me. I guess two pairs of eyes will be better than one."

Darren grabbed the crossbow and followed his grandpa. The rest of the group watched as Brad and Darren disappeared into the rolling hills and countryside.

Crawling up to the crest of a hill, Brad and Darren peeked down the other side. There was a band of about fifty well-armed people. They were resting.

"Are they the enemy?" Darren asked.

"I don't know. They aren't wearing uniforms, but that doesn't mean anything in this war. Let's work our way over to that boulder. Maybe we can hear what they're saying."

They headed toward the boulder. Darren, being younger and more agile, was able to reach cover before Brad could. When Darren looked back to see where his grandpa was, he froze. Brad was lying flat on his stomach, with a man holding a rifle to his head.

Apparently the man had not seen Darren. Darren whispered softly, "Oh God, help us."

The man was of average size, and a farmer from the looks of his clothes. He wore an old pair of bib overalls and heavy boots. *If this is the enemy,* Darren thought, *we will never be able to distinguish who we should and shouldn't trust.*

The End Is Not Yet

He heard the man speak to Brad. "Who are you? Whose side are you on?"

Brad thought for a moment. He said, "I guess my name is Old Fart."

That remark struck the man as strange, and it made him laugh.

Brad continued, "If you love our government the way it is now, then you might as well shoot me."

Then Brad heard a familiar voice. Darren was standing directly behind the man with the rifle. He had a dead aim at the man's head with the crossbow. "Put that rifle down," said Darren, "or your head will look like a speared pumpkin dripping tomato juice."

The man leaned over slowly and laid his rifle on the ground. He had been overtaken by a young whippersnapper less than half his age. He knew he was getting old, but somehow he had never noticed it until now. His farm work had kept him pretty physically and mentally fit. He was the type of man who never gave up, but here he was laying his rifle down. Should he try to regain the upper hand, or just stay calm and let things happen as they must?

His wife always told him, "Now, Fred, you stay calm. Keep your head about you." That seemed like pretty good advice in the present situation.

However, the man on the ground did spark his

interest with his "old fart" answer. Maybe things would be okay—or even better than okay—if he just waited to see who these guys really were.

Brad stood and aimed his rifle at the man. "Now who are you? What side are you on?"

The man answered, "My name is Fred Wilkins, and if you would rather die than be a supporter of our government the way it is now, then I guess that puts us both on the same side."

"My name is Brad Porter. This is my grandson, Darren Philbig. We are headed to an encampment where the soldiers have taken a lot of our family and friends. We have heard the people are being gathered as food."

"That's true," Fred said. "But it's worse than that. It's not just happening here. It's happening all over the world. The common people are being herded like cattle to slaughter.

"They are being forced to breed. It doesn't even matter if the woman is the man's sister. They don't care about the intelligence of the child, or if it is deformed. All they care about is food production. It's as if they are stockpiling food for some future disaster."

Darren interjected, "Well, why don't we cause an interruption to their food supply?"

Fred stated, "I'm with you guys!"

Darren turned to Brad and smirked. "'My name is

Old Fart'?"

Brad responded in the same mimicking tone. "'Your head will look like a speared pumpkin dripping tomato juice'? Where did that come from?"

"It's all I could think of on such short notice."

They all laughed, and the two groups joined forces. Brad and Fred made plans for the upcoming rescue.

Brad said, "Fred, you and your people concentrate on releasing the men and older boys from the cages. We will try to make it to the building complexes to release the women and children.

"We will need as much help as you can give after you're finished releasing the men. Some of those women and children won't be able to walk. We might end up having to carry quite a few of them out. Are we in agreement?"

"We sure are," said Fred.

"Diti has tried to describe the encampment and surrounding area to us, but she was pretty scared when she escaped. As young as she is, I'm not sure she was looking at it the same way you and I would. Let's keep in mind that what she described to us may not be exactly the way it is. Fear can make things appear a whole lot different than they really are. Keep a look out for other escape options in case things don't go as planned. According to Diti, it's only a few more miles."

A short time later, Brad asked Fred, "How large is your bunker?"

"We have multiple, connected bunkers. It didn't start out that way, but as we finished securing one bunker, we had a strong urge to start working on another one. So we did. We have seven large ones, all connected like a community."

"That's strange," Brad said. "That's exactly the way it was with us. We have multiple, connected bunkers also. We couldn't figure out why we were doing it, but we kept attaching more bunkers.

"Could you possibly take half the people into your bunkers? We could take the other half. We could have them write their names on a list. Then we could meet in three days at the same place you and I originally met, exchange the lists of names, and start working on getting families back together as soon as possible."

"That works for me," stated Fred.

As they got closer to the encampment, everyone started to gag from the stench. The smell of coagulated blood and feces was beyond what anyone could stand. When they were close enough to see inside the pens, they understood why. The men were standing calf-deep in blood from those who had been slaughtered.

The End Is Not Yet

The soldiers were no longer removing the men before killing them. That was taking too much time. They used an old stump for the decapitation. They built a tripod to hang the body so it would finish bleeding out.

"We need to do this right the first time. We won't get another chance," surmised Brad.

Looking at Fred, Brad continued, "There are so many to rescue. We will both have to move at the same time. That will force them to split the soldiers they have to fight us."

"Diti, you're going to have to go with us. You have to show us the way in. There won't be any time for us to make choices about where to go. Are you ready for this?" asked Brad.

"This is my chance to avenge my mom's death. I'm more than ready." She signed her commitment with a nod.

Brad requested Fred hold his people back for about ten minutes before they freed the men. This would give Brad's people a better chance to get inside the building complex in case the soldiers were alerted. Fred agreed.

With that understanding, Brad and his band of fighters headed toward the complex. They were using a half-crouched position and moving slowly to avoid detection.

Diti led them through a tunnel she had found

when she tried to get out of the basement. They worked their way up the hallways, looking in as many rooms as possible. As they found captives, a portion of the group was assigned to get them out through the tunnel to a safe place before returning to help retrieve more captives.

Fred moved his people into position. Looking at the captives, he saw how weak they all were. These were Midwestern men and boys. That meant many were farmers or ranchers. At one time they had had strong arms and backs. They were lucky. If they had been any weaker in the beginning, they might not have lived long enough to be rescued.

Some of the captives saw them approaching. He motioned for the captives to stay quiet. The captives' whispers passed throughout the pen, and soon they all knew not to give away their rescuers.

Using wire cutters in a few different locations around the pen, Fred's people cut holes large enough for the men to fit through. Slowly they started getting the men and older boys out. The stronger captives shuffled the weaker men and boys closer to the openings. Seeing this selflessness, Fred knew why they were helping these people.

Some soldiers walked out of the complex and entered the pen to select a new victim. Fred's men had to quickly hide behind some of the captives so as not to be seen. The soldiers were talking about getting together to have some beers after they got home. They were oblivious to their surroundings.

The captives crouched in fear, as they always did. However, this time it was different. The captives worked together and overtook the soldiers. After retrieving the weapons and the dreaded ax from the soldiers, the captives laid one of the soldiers over the stump. A captive took the ax and raised it. The captive stopped with the ax extended in midair. He could not bring himself to chop the soldier's head off.

He cried, "I can't do it. These men have slaughtered so many of us...and I can't kill him. What am I becoming? Am I now a weakling?" He continued to sob.

An older, white-haired man stepped out of the crowd of captives. He appeared to still have a sharp mind and a strong back. Even though he was a captive in this pen, he had continued to do exercises, just as he would have done in his own home. He had not allowed the situation to get to him. He had always held onto the hope that he would be free again. With his motivation and drive, it seemed only natural for the captives to follow this self-assured leader.

He slowly took the ax from the crying man. Reassuring his fellow captive with a soft, consoling voice, he stated, "No. You're not a weakling. You have shown yourself to be stronger than this man.

You are the kind of person we are all supposed to be. Let them be. They will get what's coming to them."

To the other captives, he ordered, "Use their handcuffs to cuff them to the tripod. Gag them so they can't alert more soldiers."

The captives continued to escape through the holes in the fence. There were so many captives, and they were very weak. It was taking a long time.

No more soldiers or police, however, seemed to be alerted. They must have been so sure their compound was secure that they weren't paying attention to what was happening.

The slaughter pen was eventually empty, except for the handcuffed soldiers. The rescued captives were taken to a place of cover, and Fred's people turned their help toward the complex.

As the women and children were carried out of the complex, Fred's people took them to safe cover in the woods. The stronger, more capable captives joined forces to help the weaker ones, the women, and the children. Everything seemed to be going smoothly and quietly.

Jules was one of the last people in the complex. He decided to do a final sweep of the rooms to ensure they hadn't missed anyone. When he turned a corner in the hallway, he found himself face-to-face with a huge, gruesome soldier. This soldier was at least six foot six, with shoulders so wide he would have had to turn sideways to fit through a door.

Jules exhaled. "Ah, shit."

The soldier, taking careful consideration of the situation, slowly pulled a combat knife from a sheath attached to his belt.

Jules, not wanting to alert more soldiers by firing a shot, readied himself for the attack. He reached down the side of his leg and slowly pulled a bowie knife from a sheath attached to his boot.

Jules had always been a lover of large knives. No matter the cost, he always had to have the best he could find. This could be the one time this knife would really pay for itself. As tough as Jules was, he knew he'd be dead meat if this guy got a hold of him.

The two started to circle each other. Both refused to break their stare. They each, in turn, lunged and swung to test the agility and readiness of the other.

Darren was getting worried. His brother should have come out of the building by now. He decided to go back in and find him. As he peered around the corner of the hallway, he saw the large soldier take a final lunge at Jules. They both collapsed to the floor. The soldier lay on top of Jules. Neither man was moving.

As Darren rushed forward to help his brother, he

heard a moan come from Jules. Jules was trying to push the huge soldier off of him. The soldier was dead. Jules's knife had found its mark. It went straight through the soldier's heart.

However, Jules was not unscathed. As Darren helped pull the soldier off Jules, he realized the soldier's knife was stuck at an angle in Jules's chest.

Darren pulled the knife out. He knew it might not be the right thing to do, but he had to. He needed to carry Jules on his back to get him out of there. "Please forgive me if this makes it worse," said Darren.

Jules, realizing the situation, remarked almost breathlessly, "Hey, man, ya gotta do what ya gotta do. Just get me out of here." He tried to force a smile. "I'll get payback later." They looked each other in the eyes and chuckled.

Darren lifted Jules up to a standing position and, turning his back to Jules, hoisted him up on his back, piggyback style. Slowly they made their way out of the encampment and joined the rest of the group. Diti gasped as she saw them coming.

Darren laid Jules on the ground and went to the first aid kit to get some bandages to wrap the wound.

Darren tried to reassure Diti. "He's okay for now, but we have to get him back to the bunker as soon as possible. Where is Harold? Get him here, fast."

The End Is Not Yet

Diti ran to get Harold, Brad, and Steve. Harold looked at the wound and wrapped Jules's chest to try to stop the bleeding. To Brad he stated, "Darren is right. We have to get him back to the bunker as soon as possible. I don't have enough supplies out here to help him much."

Knowing Jules would have to be carried back to the bunker, they made a hammock out of branches and blankets.

Darren asked, "Wouldn't Fred's bunker be the closest?"

Harold responded, "Fred's may be closer, but we don't know for sure where it is. Fred's around, helping some of the other escapees. It would take too much time to find him. We also don't know what type of medical supplies he has. I know what I've got to work with back at our bunker. Let's just go straight there."

Steve and Darren decided to carry Jules. Harold, Tonja, and Diti picked up the weapons, and the six of them headed out toward the bunker. They left the rest to reorganize the group and get the people to safety.

Brad found Fred and helped him with the escapees in the woods.

Fred introduced himself to the man who took charge of the captives in the pen. "I'm Fred Wilkins. This is Brad Porter."

"I am Cliff Smith," said the man.

"Are you related to Tabler Smith?" Brad asked.

"He is my son. Have you seen him? How is he? Did he and his family make it? My other son, Justin, was with them when this thing began. Are they okay?" He couldn't stop the questions from flying out of his mouth long enough for Brad to answer him.

"Hey, hey, slow down a bit. Tabler and Justin are here. They were helping free the women and children, so they are probably over closer to the river. He should be over beyond those trees."

Cliff didn't waste any more time talking. He took off running toward the river.

As he got closer, Justin took note and recognized the man running toward them. "Dad, we're over here," he yelled.

The three men were reunited and hugged each other.

With joy in his eyes, and trying to look behind his dad, Justin asked, "Where's Clark?"

Cliff took in a deep breath. He exhaled it slowly and told them the horrible story of their brother's death. "Clark was the first one they killed in the pen. They had taken him to the building complex. They wanted him to breed with a woman. When he refused, they brought him back to the pen and made an example of him. They brought in that old stump, made the tripod, and executed him. They were laughing while they were doing it.

"Then they decided that all the slaughtering would take place in the pen. They would pick a man out, lay him over the stump, and chop his head off. They would allow the body to flop around like a chicken with its head chopped off, while they made bets on how long the poor soul would flop and shiver. Then they would hang the body upside down from that tripod to finish bleeding out. They even made bets on how long it would take for that to happen.

"They thought making a display of what we were up against would keep us all in line, and we would do as they wanted. It only made us more resistant, so they decided they would do the honors of breeding, and we would do the honors of dying.

"They started using questions to decide who was next to be decapitated. They asked a man if he believed in God. If he said yes, it was like signing his death warrant."

Cliff spoke to those who had been in the compound with him. "We cannot let those that have died, die in vain. We must step up and help the living as much as we can, just as these people are doing."

Cliff, Tabler, and Justin joined Brad and Fred. Cliff thanked them for risking their lives to help those who had been captured.

"First we have to decide what to do with so many people," Brad said. "Then we have to decide how to do it. The longer we stay here, the more endangered everyone will be. Fred and I have already decided that we should split up the group and take them to our separate bunkers for safety, but there are a lot more people than we thought."

Cliff stated, "I know Mr. and Mrs. Faulkner were killed in their home. I saw the soldiers unload their bodies at the compound, along with some others I didn't know. Anyway, Mr. Faulkner told me once they would be safe no matter what catastrophe hit. He showed me the entrance to a bunker not far from his place." Then, as if to himself, Cliff continued, "Poor souls, I guess they didn't have time to make it to safety." He continued in a louder voice, "I didn't see the entire bunker, but I know it should be able to house some of these people."

"Let's get some of these people to our bunkers. Then a small group of us can go with you to check out the size and readiness of the Faulkners' bunker," Brad suggested to Cliff.

As he returned to the group after scouting behind them for soldiers, George was unaware of the conversation that was going on. He commented, "There are so many. How are we going to move so many through the country on foot without being seen?"

Tasha, who had been sitting and contemplating

the situation, came up with a thought. "What if we break into smaller groups? It would be safer for smaller groups to travel different routes to the bunkers. It would also be easier for a smaller group to take cover under the trees if planes are flying over. There are enough of us who know different ways back to our bunker. I'm sure Fred's people know different routes back to theirs.

"Small groups of three or four could each take groups of ten or fifteen to guide back to the bunkers. We could divide the ones that need to be carried to make it easier for everyone. That would still make groups of around twenty, but that would be better than groups of hundreds."

Brad, shooting Tasha a teasing glance, said, "I knew there was a reason your mother and I brought you girls up to be smart."

Tasha responded, "Yeah, right, Dad."

"Does something seem a bit weird to any of you?" reflected George. "With that large of a breakout, it seems strange no other soldiers were alerted beyond the few we encountered. It doesn't appear as if anyone is following us either. Why did that large soldier choose to fight Jules with a knife? Could it be he was afraid that he would alert more of *us*?"

Cliff spoke. "A couple of nights ago, I saw some covered trucks come into the compound. They loaded up some of the soldiers and left. I never dreamed they would have left so few to watch over us and continue harvesting us. I wonder where they would have taken them.

"Before that, when they would send the soldiers out on a patrol to capture more of us, they would just go in open trucks. They didn't use the heavy, large, covered ones as they did the other night. What do you think this means?"

The thought was left for each to ponder.

After dividing the group in half, Fred split his group into smaller bands. They headed in different directions, but eventually they would all go west toward their home bunker. Brad's group did the same, heading in a more southerly direction. They arrived at the bunkers safely without any incidents.

After everyone was fed, it was time to start the list of everyone in the bunker. While the paper was being passed around, Brad, George, Tabler, and Cliff made plans to reach the Faulkners' bunker.

Harold reported that Jules would be okay. Miraculously, the knife missed any vital organs. It had taken a while to stop the bleeding, but he would be fine. He just needed to rest.

Sue made it her priority to keep an eye on the wound, so it wouldn't get infected.

With the good news about Jules, Steve and Darren decided it would be okay for them to tag along with the others to see what the Faulkners' bunker looked like.

Cliff led them to a large mound of earth with brush and vines growing over it. It was sloped to conceal a doorway. Cliff found the entrance to the bunker rather quickly. The question was how to open it. They searched the area for some type of lever or anything that might cause the doorway to open up.

Rather perturbed he couldn't remember how Mr. Faulkner opened the doorway, Cliff started pacing.

"You keep that up," Darren said, "and you'll wear a hole in the ground. We'll be in China before we're in that bunker."

As if a light bulb went on in his brain, Cliff stated, "That's it! He paced. He went straight up here."

Cliff pointed. "He stepped about three paces left, then three paces right, and then back to the left. He went to the right and left twice. I didn't think anything of it. I thought maybe he was looking for something."

Mr. Faulkner had hidden an eyebeam unit in the brush next to the opening to the bunker. The only way to trigger the beam to open the bunker was to make the required amount of passes in front of the beam. Cliff didn't know it, but it didn't matter how many paces he made, or which direction he went first. Cliff tried it. A doorway popped open about two inches. He just had to reach his hand in and pull it the rest of the way open.

Inside it was just like the Porter bunker. This bunker was well stocked with everything. There was even a bunker set up like a hospital. One bunker was food and supplies storage. Another bunker contained all sorts of weaponry, ammunition, surveillance cameras, binoculars, and whatever else would be needed to keep this home safe. The rest of the bunkers were housing units. It was as if they weren't just planning for themselves.

After three days had passed, Fred and Brad met to exchange the lists of names. Brad told Fred the good news about the Faulkners' bunker. They could now divide the two groups into three.

The first order of business was to get the families back together. Cliff would then lead the third group and settle them in at the new bunker.

Everyone was told about the three places. The people were allowed to choose if they wanted to stay in the bunker or move to another one. When all was said and done, the three groups were divided equally. Friends and families were reunited, and everyone was okay with where they were to live.

Strangers were not strangers anymore. They were brethren with closer ties than they ever would have imagined possible.

***

Later, when Jules was able to get up again, he walked from his sleeping area to the kitchen. He could hear someone crying softly. He followed the sound into one of the storage bunkers. It was Diti.

"What's the matter, Diti?" His heart went out to her because she had been through so much, but it didn't stop her from giving her all to help those who needed it so badly.

"I didn't really expect to find my two little sisters," she said. "I kind of knew they were dead, but I held out such hope to find my father and brothers. I don't know what to do without them. I'll be all alone now," Diti muttered.

Jules wasn't sure what to say. He stepped closer to Diti and put his arms around her. She laid her head on his shoulder.

"You'll be okay, Diti. You can lean on me. I won't ever leave you. My family won't leave you either."

Chapter 8

The Movement

The president of the United States was a self-motivated man. After he took office, he started campaigning for new changes. Some of the changes he wanted to make dealt with job security. He spoke directly to the people, giving them hope that he could change things for the better. He led them to believe he was referring to their jobs regarding better pay, insurance, and work practices.

He was able to speak so eloquently that he had the common people believing he was doing everything he could to help them. In the end, it meant that he would be the recipient of paid vacations, unlimited travel on Air Force One, new cars, and free housing for him, his family, and his future families, for the rest of their lives. This would all be paid by the taxpayers. He had his own agenda, and it didn't include helping those less fortunate than he.

A majority of the congressmen believed in him. The initial changes had been small, and the changes regarding where the money came from didn't seem to really hurt anyone. A few dollars out of this fund. A few dollars out of that fund.

Some of the congressmen saw what was coming and tried to counter his changes. Soon the people were voting those congressmen out of office. With the only congressmen left being total supporters of the president, he had unwritten power to conduct business as he saw fit. He had gained the confidence of the people by lying to them. He knew how to mix just enough truth into his messages to make them believable.

He didn't know the meaning of patriotism. Most people didn't notice he would not salute the flag, and he didn't remove his cap when they were playing the national anthem at a baseball game.

The president called a special meeting. He said it was mandatory for the vice president, the speaker of the house, the chiefs of staff, and his cabinet members to attend. The meeting was to begin promptly at 0800 hours in the Oval Office.

"Mr. President, the safety of our country is jeopardized. As you ordered, many troops have been deployed to Mexico, Canada, and Latin

America to overtake those countries and make them ours. The simultaneous deployment of so many troops, however, has left our homeland security at risk," reported Secretary of Defense John Silvers.

Secretary of Agriculture Bud Corley interjected, "We have to consider the food supply. The people from all those countries will deplete their food supply, and ours, in no time."

The president was standing in front of the window where he had once looked out at the White House rose garden. He was now gazing at an encampment built to hold his private stock.

"Our food supply will never be depleted." He turned his head toward Bud Corley and, with a sly smirk, said, "At least not for those of us who count."

To Bud, that seemed like a strange statement for the president to say. After all, wasn't he supposed to be *for* the people? That food supply he was looking at was supposed to be for everyone. Now Bud wondered if what he had been told about those people having been convicted of treason, and sent here for confinement, was really true.

John Silvers said, "Maybe we should call some of our soldiers back. It has been reported that Russia and China are having private talks. It appears they might be planning to take over the United States."

"Don't worry so much. I have a handle on this

situation. Russia and China are in my pocket," said the president. "We will take over Mexico, Canada, and Latin America as planned."

"Mr. President, it is true. Our informants have advised me that China is pushing Russia to side against us. I have also been informed that, after they overtake us, China has plans to turn against Russia. China wants to be the kingpin. They want us all under their thumb," reported National Security Advisor William Abner.

"I cannot confirm or deny any of this. The heads of both China and Russia have refused to speak with me," said Secretary of State James Brushnell.

James Brushnell could generally smell when something wasn't right, and things were starting to stink. He had bad vibes about China and Russia being so closemouthed with him. Worse than that, he could sense the president was not being completely honest about everything.

He had been raised to be straightforward about things, especially if it was for the good of other people. The people of other countries counted on him to be straight with them to keep camaraderie alive. He thought that was why he had been given this position. Lately he had begun to wonder if that was the real reason, or if the president thought he would just blindly do as he was told.

"I told you. I have China and Russia in my pocket. They would not dare go against me," responded the president with an all-knowing look on his face. He did not want to give out too much information. It would all be over soon.

The doors burst open. Chinese and Russian soldiers flooded the room.

They had taken over the secret service and now held Todd Blancher, the director, at gunpoint. They used their rifles to push him toward the president. Without turning around or looking back, the soldiers separated to make an aisle for General Tseng.

General Tseng had proven to be very ruthless.

He had been cold-blooded, even as a young boy. When he was ten years old, he told his younger brother to carry his books to school. His brother refused. General Tseng pulled out a pocketknife, stabbed him in the heart, and threw his brother's body in an old abandoned well. His brother was never found.

In his early career as a soldier, he had his comrades so afraid of him, they would take the fall for any of his misdoings. They knew that if they didn't, they wouldn't live to see the morning.

Any heroics were attributed to Tseng. This gave Tseng a shining military record. He was always the one being promoted.

"This was a lot easier than I could have wished for," said General Tseng. "Thank you for your help,

The End Is Not Yet

Mr. President. Having the troops out of the country was a spark of sheer genius. You will be at my table for dinner this evening. Yes? It has been a long day." General Tseng sighed as if he was bored.

James Brushnell glared at the president with anger and disbelief. "You've got them in your pocket? It looks more as if they've got you in theirs. You betrayed us for them? How can you live with yourself?"

As if indignant such a question could be asked of him, the president responded with laughter. Then he said, "Obviously better than you can!"

Following the general out of the room, the president passed a Russian soldier. Without stopping, he ordered, "Shoot him." The president continued toward the door. Without looking back, he listened for the gunshot. As he was going through the door, he heard it and smiled. "What insolence," he muttered to himself.

In the hallway, outside of the office, the president was handcuffed by some Chinese soldiers. He would be *served* at the General's table that evening.

The rest of the heads in the room were taken captive and put in the encampments they had subjected their fellow Americans to. They would be next on the chopping block.

***

The timing of the president's and Russia's first combined attacks had to be strategic. The devastation was to start at 0830 hours. The attacks could not begin until the president was already in his special meeting.

A group of American soldiers happened to be going through a meadow. They were cutting across country instead of sticking to the roads. They had not captured many renegades, and they thought this would increase their chances of finding them.

Their commanding officers were getting upset. There was a quota, and they were not achieving it. Their orders were to bring in at least fifty renegades each time they were sent out. They had failed to achieve this on their last two reconnaissance missions.

This would be their final chance. If they didn't bring in the number of renegades required, they would be used to make up the difference. Their families would also be used to make up any lacking numbers.

The rest of the cabinet didn't know it, but this was what the president meant when he said, "Our food supply will never be depleted—at least not for those of us who count."

The lieutenant heard the sound of planes in the distance. "Listen. Doesn't that sound like Russian MiGs? I wonder why they are crossing our airspace. We are supposed to be friendly with Russia."

The End Is Not Yet

Soon the MiGs were in view, and they started shooting at the soldiers.

Some of the soldiers jerked their heads in the direction of the MiGs and fell to the ground. Others were so startled they just stood there and allowed themselves to be shot down, without exhibiting the slightest reflex to fight back or run for cover.

The soldiers jumped up and started running. They ran fast, jumping over their fellow fallen soldiers and hoping to reach safety among the trees in the woods. None of them made it.

The MiGs came in like a flock of birds descending on the soldiers. They killed the soldiers and then flew off into the horizon as if they had just been out for a joyride.

Then the real birds came. There were flocks of eagles, hawks, vultures, ravens, crows, and every type of scavenger bird created by God. They came to feast on the bodies of the fallen soldiers.

This was happening everywhere across the United States. Russian Bear bombers headed toward the major cities of each state, and their MiGs shot at anything that moved.

Russian and Chinese soldiers were taking over all the compounds. They realized they had adversaries in the countryside when they found some of the encampments empty. They started a large-scale search for any and all enemies of the Chinese and Russian regime.

When General Tseng heard this news, he ordered any discovered enemies to be tortured. "The torturing will consist of cutting large hunks of meat from their bodies while keeping them alive. The meat will be ground into hamburger before their very eyes.

They will tell us where the rest of their fellow comrades are hiding. If they do not give up that information, force them to eat their own flesh, and then cut off more. They will speak."

The news travelled fast between the many bunkers across the United States.

Those from the encampments swore the soldiers would not go unpunished for what they had done, and for what they were about to do. Now the bunker people had additional enemies. They would have to fight the Chinese and the Russians as well. They gathered as much ammunition as they could, in readiness for their fight for freedom. They snuck out of the bunkers to make traps. They dug holes. In the Midwest, they pointed sharpened tree limbs straight up and covered them with small branches and leaves. To some, these were known as punji sticks. To others they were just called "death for the evildoers." In the South they filled the holes with deadly snakes.

Trees that would bend without breaking were pulled down and tied off. Lassos were attached to them. Fallen leaves and twigs covered the lassos.

The End Is Not Yet

When unsuspecting soldiers stepped into the lasso, it would break the tie that held the tree. The tree would snap itself upright, pulling the soldier up and back, and flinging him or her into a wall with sharpened wooden stakes mounted in it, as the ancient Japanese had done. The newer version of this trap had acid-filled glass jars. When the soldiers tripped the lassos, the soldiers were flung back, along with the jars. These jars would break and spill acid in the soldiers' faces.

The bunker people didn't have land mines, so they devised string traps across the ground. When the soldiers caught their feet on the strings, the contraption pulled the pins on the grenades that had been attached to them.

Hidden among the trees, and covered with extra bushes, were 240-volt generators. Holes were dug close to low-hanging branches on trees and covered to appear as if they were just puddles. The holes had to be deep enough so the soldiers would reach for the low-hanging branches to pull themselves out of the would-be grave. Hot and neutral wires were strung from the generators to the low-hanging branches. When the soldiers grabbed the branches, they unwittingly grabbed the wires.

To avoid the noise of the generator, the bunker people decided that some of Sitting Bull's tactics from Little Bighorn would work well. They allowed a soldier to chase them into the woods with enough distance between them so the bunker people could hide. One person hid near the generator. After the soldier fell into the trap, the bunker person came out of hiding and turned on the generator. The soldier grabbed the low branch and was electrocuted.

They laid booby traps everywhere, using as many different types of traps as they could devise. The word was passed from bunker to bunker about what everyone should watch for when traveling through the woods.

The fighting continued like this. The bunker people killed soldiers with traps. The soldiers killed bunker people by torture, mutilation, and decapitation. There was so much blood, and nobody bothered to bury the dead.

When a person looked out across a plain or a meadow, all he or she could see were bodies fallen over bodies…and the birds. Masses of birds of all kinds had gathered and were feeding on the carcasses of those killed.

The rivers ran red from so many dead. Even when it rained, the rain would fall high in the mountains, and push more blood down to the lowlands.

It was like this all over the world. Each nation was fighting another nation, and there was internal fighting. There were no alliances. The only alliances left were the ones made by those who lived in the bunker communities. Even some of those alliances were starting to wither as the communities became increasingly self-indulgent.

When bunker people with vengeful hearts were caught, they would give up the location of other bunkers to save their lives. In the end, there were only a few bunker communities that continued to stand together and pledged that life would be good again...someday.

***

"Shouldn't we be helping to fight this war?" asked Jules. "We should be fighting out there instead of hiding in here."

Debbie looked at her grandson with sad eyes. "We are not hiding in here. The Lord has provided this place of refuge for us. We are living the way we are supposed to be living for now. We will have to make a stand one day, but that day hasn't come yet.

"Do you think those people out there are fighting for any other reason than revenge? They started out fighting for survival, but now they are fighting out of hate. The more they fight, the more their hearts are being hardened. They just want to get back at the soldiers.

"The Bible stated this would happen. We need to accept that. We have to try to keep our hearts from hardening. We can't allow hatred to rule us. Let me read a couple verses to you."

She took her Bible from the bookshelf, opened it, and found the scriptures she wanted to read. She began with Revelation 13:10:

> He who leads into captivity shall go into captivity; he who kills with the sword must be killed with the sword.

She then turned to Romans 12:19-21:

> Beloved, do not avenge yourselves, but *rather* give place to wrath; for it is written, "Vengeance is mine, I will repay," says the Lord. Therefore "If your enemy is hungry, feed him; If he is thirsty, give him a drink; For in so doing you will heap coals of fire on his head." Do not be overcome by evil, but overcome evil with good.

"That means we need to show compassion for our fellow man. Please stay out of their fighting." Debbie looked away, as if that was all her heart would allow her to say. Deep inside she was thinking of how her mother had always made sure that she and her siblings went to church.

As Debbie grew older, she drifted between going to church and going to bars. She had gone back and forth from the right side of life to the wild side of life, but she never lost her love of the Lord.

Meeting Brad was one of the best things that ever happened to her. She had prayed for God to send someone who would truly love her, and God had answered her prayers. Why hadn't that been enough to get her reading her Bible more, and following its teachings?

She and Brad both believed in God, but somehow going to church had never become part of their lives. They had sometimes read the Bible, but even that was done separately—and not very often.

When her girls were young, Debbie made sure they attended church consistently for a while. As time passed, though, she forgot about church again. Now she didn't know if her grandchildren have ever been in church. They were all good kids, but would that be enough to get them to heaven? They would need to love the Lord in their own right.

When she looked at herself, she thought of when the Lord said, "I know your works, that you are neither cold nor hot. I could wish that you were cold or hot. So then, because you are lukewarm, and neither cold nor hot, I will vomit you out of My mouth."

Why did it take the coming of the last days before Debbie finally understood that God was real? Why did all these things that had been foretold have to happen before she opened her eyes and her heart to the truth? Now she could only pray that she had enough faith in God to persevere, if she was ever put to the test.

She prayed that God would forgive her. The Bible said He would, but she had to truly believe it, and believe in Him. She had enough knowledge of the

Bible to know these were the last days; but was it too late for her, her family, and their friends?

It is never too late for those who believe, she thought.

She remembered Revelation 3:20-21:

"Behold, I stand at the door and knock. If anyone hears My voice and opens the door, I will come in to him and dine with him, and he with Me. To him who overcomes I will grant to sit with Me on My throne, as I also overcame and sat down with My Father on His throne."

Chapter 9

Devastation and Plagues

Devastation and plagues advanced throughout the land. In every country there was something that could hinder or kill the people. There was no place to hide.

The soldier stepped down from the bus that had brought him home to Beijing, China. He had done well during his last tour of combat and had secured a furlough to go home for the weekend. He grabbed his duffel bag and strolled up the city street. He stopped to talk to a little girl playing outside her home. "Hi, Xian-li! Here. I have a gift for you." He gave her a leftover candy bar from his tour of duty. He waved good-bye and continued walking up the street toward his home.

Later, Xian-li Chang and Bai Wong were playing happily together in Bai Wong's tiny home. The war had not affected the two young, fun-loving girls.

They had been protected because they were family members of the high regime.

They were pretending to be ballerinas. Xian-li, as hard as she tried, could not balance on her toes. The higher she tried to get, the more she would topple over. This made Bai laugh. Bai then felt the need to show her little friend how it was done. Surprisingly, Bai was able to do it once, before she toppled over too. Ultimately they found themselves laughing as they picked themselves up off the floor.

Xena, Bai's mother, said, "Xian-li, you go home now. It is time for us to eat our supper."

Xian-li, having been brought up to respond to orders immediately and without question, graciously thanked Mrs. Wong for allowing her to play with Bai, and headed home. She knew it would be suppertime at her house too.

As the Wong family gathered around the table to eat, Bai started to feel uneasy. She stood beside the table, but started to sway. She grabbed for her mother, who was standing beside her, but she missed. Her brother, Meng, who had been standing on the opposite side of Bai, was able to catch her before she fell to the floor.

"Bai, what is the matter?" asked her mother.

"I don't know. I was fine when I was playing with Xian-li. Now I feel…" Her words faded away as she passed out and fell into Meng's arms.

The End Is Not Yet

"Meng. Go get Dr. Ho. Now!" Xena yelled to her son.

Marrin took his daughter from Meng and carried her to the bedroom. He gave her a kiss on her forehead as he pulled the blankets up around her. *I wonder what is wrong with her*, he thought. *Maybe she just played too hard with her friend.*

It was not long before Dr. Ho arrived. He was led into the bedroom, where little Bai was curled up in the fetal position in her bed. She was drenched in sweat that poured from her weakened body. The doctor rolled Bai flat on her back so he could examine her. He noticed some strange lesions on her face. "What was she doing?" said Dr. Ho. "Has she gotten into a fight?"

Annoyed that the doctor would ask such a question, Xena responded, "Our little girl does not fight. She was raised properly. She was only playing ballerina with her friend who lives down the street."

Soon, Marrin started to feel woozy too. "I think I will go lie down before I fall over as well," he said.

He stumbled trying to walk to his bed. He barely made it before he collapsed. He was starting to sweat profusely. Welts began to form on his face.

Dr. Ho tried to support little Bai as she attempted to sit up. She slumped back and quietly died.

Xena screamed. "What has happened? You need

to help her. She must be okay. She just *has* to be okay."

The doctor put his arm around Xena's shoulder. He told her there wasn't anything more he could do for her daughter. He then started spouting orders. "Everything in this home must be sanitized. The sheets, blankets, pillows, and mattress of Bai's bed must be burned."

He turned to Marrin, but Marrin died before the doctor had a chance to examine him.

"Their bodies will need to be burned, but first I will need to do some test to find out what this is. You do as I said. Do not try to save anything I told you to burn. Do this immediately. Where is the other little girl's home? I will need to check on her and her family, to see if they are ill too."

Xena told the doctor where Xian-li lived. He quickly left the Wongs' home.

As he closed the door behind the doctor, Meng turned to his mother. "I don't feel so well..."

Dr. Ho knocked on the door of the home of little Xian-li Chang. Xian-li's older brother opened it. He had been crying. Everyone was crying.

The doctor was too late. Xian-li's limp body lay on the couch.

Dr. Ho walked over to the little girl. A tear started to fall from his eye. "What can this be?" he said.

The End Is Not Yet

He ordered the Chang family to sanitize or burn everything Xian-li had come in contact with. He also gave them the bad news that Xian-li's body would have to be burned immediately.

As the doctor left the Chang home, he wondered how many of them would still be alive in the morning. When he got back to his office, he ordered the removal of the dead bodies from the Wong and Chang homes. He cautioned the ambulance workers to use hazardous protection outfits.

Dr. Ho sat at his desk and covered his face with his palms. When his assistant entered his office to let him know the bodies were being transported, he uncovered his face. His assistant could see the worry in his eyes. The two had worked together for many years. She knew how to read the doctor. She knew it was not her place to ask, but she wondered what the doctor was so worried about. She silently reached out and touched the top of his hand in sympathy.

Without rising from his seat, the doctor looked directly into her eyes. He was afraid to frighten her, but he was also afraid to keep from her what he knew would eventually affect everyone.

He spoke softly. "I hope our people transporting those bodies are using the protection I told them to. I believe we have an epidemic, and it is spreading fast. It only takes a few hours from the point of contact for the person to die."

The doctor loosened his tie from around his neck. He was starting to sweat profusely.

Seeing that Dr. Ho was becoming ill, his assistant called for another doctor to examine him. Soon she, too, began to feel unstable, and sat down.

The ambulance arrived at Dr. Ho's office with the bodies. Dr. Ho's assistant got up from the chair to peer out the window at the ambulance. She saw them carry the bodies into the clinic. The bodies were not covered well, and the ambulance workers hadn't even put on rubber gloves, much less hazardous protection suits.

This was their last transport of the day. Soon they would be going home to their families.

The new doctor arrived but as much as he tried to revive Dr. Ho, it was no use. Dr. Ho passed away without saying one word about the epidemic that was about to tear the city apart.

The assistant sat in her chair in the outer office. She wiped her forehead as she started to sweat profusely. She felt a welt developing on her face.

***

In a bunker near the city of Edmonton, Canada, Sammy Mosier sat at the dining table. He was bored, so he was trying to paint a picture to keep his mind occupied. He was painting a picture of the devastation he had witnessed when he was out with the group on a raid. His group often did raids, and he enjoyed them. He was always one of the first to volunteer when they were going on a manhunt.

His eighteen years made him just young enough to see excitement in such atrocities, and just old enough to struggle within his soul about whether they were right or wrong. He painted pictures to hide his emotional frailty on the subject. With the way he acted and the pictures he painted, no one ever questioned his manhood.

The previous night, his group had gone on a raid. They came across some soldiers. They decided it was time to get revenge on those soldiers. They lured the soldiers into a clearing where they had rope traps hidden. The soldiers were caught in the traps. They were alive and well until the bunker people decided differently. They never gave them a chance. They held out the limbs of some of the soldiers and chopped them off with dull axes. Some of the soldiers were tied in crisscross fashion between bent-over trees. As the taut ropes were cut, the trees regained their upright position and tore the soldiers in half.

Sammy started to rub his throat. He could feel a burning dryness starting to build inside of it. "Mom, I think I might be catching the flu or something," he said.

His mom walked over to him. Lucille felt her

son's forehead to see if he was getting a fever. He appeared to be okay.

She looked at the picture her son was painting. "Where did you get the idea to paint this?" she said.

"It is a painting of what we did to those rotten soldiers last night," he remarked boastfully. He avoided looking into his mother's eyes.

Lucille affirmed his gallantry. "You guys are doing a great job. The soldiers deserve it. Keep up the good work."

About twenty minutes later, she noticed Sammy had laid his head on his arms on the table. She told him to lie in his bunk so she could set the table for supper, but he was dead.

Sammy's father had gone into the social room to sit in his chair and read a book while he waited for supper.

Lucille ran to the boy's father. "Todd, something has happened. Sammy is dead."

Seeing her husband, she stopped and put her hands over her mouth. Todd had also gone out on the raid the night before. He too was dead.

Angela, Sammy's twelve-year-old sister, called her mom to the sleeping room. "Mom, I think I'm getting a sore throat."

She had not gone out on the raid.

The End Is Not Yet

***

Maria Sanchez had lived in Mexico all her life. She had owned a small restaurant. As times became harder, business slowed down, and she was forced to sell it. Because she was a great cook, she was hired to cook for the Mexican army.

One day as she was busy making supper for the soldiers, her nose started to bleed. She wiped it away, tilted her head back, and pinched the upper part of her nose in an effort to make it stop bleeding. After she got it to stop, she washed her hands and continued making supper.

Simultaneously a soldier was taking a shower before going to the mess hall for supper. He reached for the soap. His nose started gushing blood. He reached for a washcloth to stop the bleeding. He tilted his head back. His nose continued to bleed. It was unstoppable. He leaned against the shower wall for support. As he began to lose his strength, he slowly slid down the shower wall until he was sitting on the floor. He was getting so weak, he could not even call for help. He died.

The shower was still running. The water circulated the blood around the drain in the shower floor. No one was there to notice.

Back in the kitchen, Maria Sanchez stirred the chili. Her nose started to bleed again. She couldn't catch the blood fast enough. Some blood fell into the chili. She quickly moved away from the stove and grabbed a towel. She couldn't stop her nose from bleeding this time. She slowly lost her strength, stumbled to the floor, and died.

Servers entered the kitchen to help set up for supper. They found Maria sprawled out on the floor. They called for medical assistance. It was determined Maria died from natural causes. They removed her body from the kitchen, and the servers took over the rest of the meal preparation. They stirred the chili and dished it up into the bowls to be served to the soldiers.

***

In the backroom of a restaurant in Berlin, Brigadier Hans Bergmann met with a group of his most trusted commandants and subordinates.

"We have to try to regain control of our country from the Chinese and Russians. We can no longer trust our country's leader. He is on their side."

To the subordinates, he declared, "You will be the heroes if you do this. You must instill in your men that they must not lay down their weapons. They must not surrender. They must defeat the enemy.

"Those of us who are higher ranking will be able to help you best by finding out exactly what our leader is up to, and secretly keeping you posted. If any brigadier generals, or higher, find out what we are doing we will all be shot. We have devised a plan for you to follow. You will instruct your men regarding what they are to do. You will need to follow the plan to a T. After we have secured control of our country, you will be decorated for your heroics, and we will all celebrate."

Suddenly the commandant started to feel an itching sensation on his arms. Soon he was scratching his face. He started to shake, and he sat down in his chair. He died.

Others in the meeting started to itch. They started to shake. Soon they, too, were dead.

Those who still felt fine ordered the bodies of the dead to be removed from the room. They continued with the meeting. As the meeting concluded, they went to be with their families. Once again in the safety of their homes, they took comfort in the closeness of their families.

Shortly afterward, they all began to itch.

***

In all of Africa, India, and Latin America, there was no water. The rivers were mere sand paths traveling off in the distance. Lake Victoria in Africa—once known as the largest freshwater lake in the world—was turning into a dust bowl. Remains of humans and animals lay where they died from thirst along the lake's edge.

There was no such thing as a rain forest anymore. There was nothing. It was all destitute and dry. Without the rain forests to assist in the production of oxygen, people wondered how there would be enough oxygen to sustain life. Other parts of the world would ultimately feel the effects. Remaining plant life started to wither. Soon there wouldn't be food of any kind. Fires ignited in some countries due to extreme heat and dryness. The droughts continued to cause all kinds of devastation.

Abanobi, an African hunter, lived in a remote African village. He had led many safaris in his lifetime. He knew what to expect from the wild animals. He was fearless where lions were concerned. He could read the signs to track the animals. He could foresee when the animals tried tricks such as doubling back to entrap him. He could turn the tables on them, and he would bag his meat. He was known as the great hunter who would always bring home meat for the tribe.

He knew the ways to survive in Africa, and how to keep his family safe and healthy, but this drought was making everything different. The vegetation he normally gathered was gone. Everything was withering up and dying.

All of the animals, wild or domestic, were acting differently. The lions, especially, were becoming very bold. The lions had never ventured too close to the villages. They had used the grassy plains for cover to stalk their prey, but now there weren't any grassy plains.

The End Is Not Yet

Abanobi had to do something to get water to the village. He would have to go to Lake Victoria for some freshwater to bring back to the village. He had no way of knowing about the conditions around Lake Victoria.

He gathered up the menfolk of the village. They filled two old flatbed trucks with empty water barrels. The trucks had side rails, so they would be good for transporting the water barrels. All the young men with strong backs would travel with the trucks to help fill the barrels and reload them onto the trucks. The elderly men would stay behind to protect the village while the young tribesmen were gone.

Abanobi gave his wife, Chalondra, a hug. "Take care of the children. Yafeu and I will be back as soon as we can. And then we will have enough water for everyone."

Chalondra gave Abanobi a kiss for luck and gave Yafeu, her eldest son, a hug. "You stay safe, and come back to us. With or without water. We love you."

Abanobi spoke to Da'ron, his second-oldest son. "You stay sharp. Keep your mother and little brother and sisters safe."

With a wave to the family, Abanobi and Yafeu climbed into the truck and headed to the central water house. There they met up with the other men that would make the trip to Lake Victoria.

Some of the men grabbed the village's few rifles, and others collected their spears. There wasn't enough room for everyone to ride inside the truck, so some of the younger men climbed in the back of the trucks to ride beside the barrels. Yafeu gave up his cab seat to an older huntsman and climbed up on the back with his friends. The trucks were now ready.

With Abanobi driving the lead truck, they headed out of the village. They were only about five miles out of the village when they came upon four lions in the middle of the road. The lions would not move. They paced back and forth across the road, as if daring the trucks to pass. There were numerous lions lying low in the distance. They were slowly moving around to encircle the two trucks. Then they started moving in closer to the trucks. They were readying themselves to pounce when the moment was right.

Abanobi tried to move the truck slowly forward to urge the lions to back away. The lions kept their steady pace back and forth. One lion from the outer perimeter crept closer and lunged toward the second truck. A tribesman raised his rifle and shot it. It was a good hit. The lion was dead.

Then a lioness lunged from the rear. She was able to grab one of the men's legs. She dragged him off the truck. Even though he had a spear, it did him no good. The lioness had him by the throat, and in seconds the man was dead.

The End Is Not Yet

The lions moved closer with each strike. Both trucks were under attack, and the lions were everywhere.

When Abanobi saw a lioness grab Yafeu, he grabbed his rifle, jumped out of the cab, and turned to aim his rifle. Abanobi never raised the rifle. A lioness had him by the back of the neck.

There would be no water for the village.

After the trucks left the village, Chalondra took the rest of the children inside their home. She had turned to close the door when she saw a lioness jump on the back of Dakari, a village elder left behind to protect the village.

As other village elders ran to Dakari's aid, lions attacked them too.

Chalondra looked up and down the street. There were lions everywhere. Chalondra watched as a lion jumped through a window of a house. The lion later came out of the house with a human arm in its mouth.

Moving as quickly as possible, Chalondra stashed her three youngest children on the ceiling beams, hoping that the lions would not be able to reach them. She told the children to stay quiet no matter what happened. She took a machete down from its home on the wall and handed it to Da'ron. "Use this as accurately as you can," she said. "You will only get one try."

She grabbed the butcher knife she had been using to cook their supper and clutched it tightly in her hands. She was not about to let anything pry it from her fingers.

They were as ready as they were ever going to be. They watched the front windows.

They heard something behind them. They turned around as three lionesses came in through the windows in the back of the house.

Not taking his eyes off the lionesses, Da'ron quietly and solemnly asked, "Mama, is this it?"

Chalondra knew exactly what he meant. Not wanting to answer but having always been truthful with her children, she quietly answered, "Yes, Da'ron. I believe it is."

The lionesses lunged at the mother and son. The lionesses made short work of killing them. They began to tear the meat apart. They paid no attention to the children in the rafters. They dragged the bodies of Chalondra and Da'ron into the streets to provide food for the lions.

Then they returned to the house. One lioness leaped toward the ceiling beams. This surprised five-year-old Nadia. She jerked back. As she did so, the hem of her dress fell below the beam. It was just low enough that, with the lioness's next lunge, its claws caught it. The lioness yanked the little girl down.

The End Is Not Yet

At that same moment, Nadia's seven-year-old brother, Yami, tried to grab her to keep her from falling. He lost his balance and fell with her.

This left three-year-old Na'zyia sitting on the beam, crying. It wouldn't matter if the lions got her or not. She was about to die from thirst.

A few days later, the village was quiet. There were dead bodies, and parts of dead bodies, everywhere.

The lions and lionesses lay dead in the streets. They had found food, but no water.

***

In the United States, the drought was not quite as bad...yet.

"Steve, I turned the water on, but I can't get any. You don't suppose we could be out of water, do you?" asked Tonja.

Steve answered, "I wouldn't think so. We have a pretty large lake on this property. Let me take a look at it." He tried to turn on the water. "You can see the shaft turning, but there's no water being discharged from the pump." He disassembled the pump to find why it wasn't pumping water properly. The impeller seemed to be worn out.

Brad entered the kitchen area. "What's up? Do we have a problem?"

Thinking more about the problem then

answering Brad's question, Steve said, "Why would the impeller be worn out on the pump? That means the pump was working harder to get water, doesn't it?"

Brad stated, "We haven't had any rain this summer. Maybe the water is low in the lake. It's been hot outside. We just don't feel it so much because we're in here. If you look at the monitors, nothing seems to be growing as it should. Let's get the pump out of the pump house. We can take a look at the lake at the same time."

Steve and Brad prepared themselves to go out. They snuck over to the pump house. After looking at the pump, Brad stated, "This one will never do. With no one living in the farmhouse in the wintertime, there wasn't any heat turned on in the pump house. The water froze. That caused the casing to crack, and it split the pump's impeller."

Steve spoke hesitantly, "We might be able to find a pump at one of the farms around here, but we can't be sure it'll work. The only way we can be sure about fixing this problem is to get a pump repair kit from the plumbing supply store in town."

"That about sums it up, and seeing as how we won't be able to buy one from them, I guess we'll have to scrounge one from them," Brad said.

They took a look at the lake on the way back to the bunker. It was down two-thirds from what it should be. The grass and weeds were either brown or totally nonexistent.

Brad stated, "If rain doesn't come soon, we may not need a pump."

Sitting at the table when Steve and Brad entered the bunker, Debbie asked how things looked outside, and what the final decision was regarding the water pump.

Steve answered, "It appears we will be making a trip to town. We will need a repair kit to fix it."

Looking at the wrinkles that were showing on her husband's face, and the gray that was making his once soft, shiny hair appear lifeless and dull, Debbie didn't want him to make this hard, fast trip to town.

"I hate to say this, dear, but the years are getting the better of you. Maybe you should let the younger ones go. They would be able to get there and back the fastest. Right now we have enough water in storage to last for a few days, but it won't last long with all the people here. We will need that pump fixed as soon as possible. Don't you agree?" asked Debbie.

"You hate to say it, and I hate to admit it, but I guess you're right," Brad said.

Steve, George, Darren, and Jules decided they would make the trip to town to get the water pump repair kit.

George stated, "This trip might be easier than we

think. I heard they were allowing people to return to their homes and their jobs if they were willing to live under the government restrictions of how much food and supplies they kept. But they had to give up their weapons and ammo if they acquired any. Maybe we can walk around, and no one will notice us."

Ray Chandler was a rowdy young man who had come to the bunker from the encampment. In the years before the crisis, he'd had a few squabbles with the law, but he had tried to be a better person and do what was expected of him by society.

Ray inquired, "Do any of you know how to pick a lock or disarm a security system?"

The four who were preparing to go out looked at each other.

"I thought not. You need me to go along. You see, I do have those skills. If the soldiers are still around town, they might have set the security alarms on some of the buildings to warn them in case people like us happen to show up," Ray suggested.

"Okay, you can come. Do you know how to shoot a gun?" asked Steve.

"I've shot a few in my day. I'm not great at it, but I think I can do what needs to be done," answered Ray.

The five of them packed up their weapons and

enough food for a two-day trip. When everything was ready, they set out for town.

When they arrived, they had to stay in the shadows and watch for any movement. They worked their way to Hansel's Plumbing Supply on the east side of town. They wouldn't need Ray's skills there. Half of the building had been destroyed.

"The soldiers must have been trying to prove a point to someone," whispered Jules. "Or maybe they want to be able to keep an eye on these types of supplies, considering the only other plumbing supply in town is right across from the police station. The rumor is the soldiers have taken control of the station and killed any police officers who resisted."

"There's nothing else we can do but go to Franklin's Plumbing. We have to get a pump," stated George.

A river used to run through the town and flow behind Franklin's Plumbing. Now the river was just a deep, wide ditch. Franklin had built his store's rear parking lot so it ran close to the embankment of that river. He had been trying to make use of as much available parking space as possible.

The five travelled through the alleyways to avoid being seen. They used the dried-up riverbed and embankment to crawl as close to the building as possible without being seen by soldiers.

They made it. They were at the back door of the building, and Ray worked his magic. They were able to get inside without any alarms going off. They easily found a water pump repair kit. They also grabbed a few extra things they might need in the future.

Ray crept up to the storefront to peek out the windows. He wanted to see if there were any soldiers in the streets. Steve, George, Jules, and Darren headed out the back door.

"Come on, Ray. We don't want to risk getting caught in here. If we get caught taking a water pump, they'll torture us to find out why we need one, and the family still won't have any water. Come on." Darren almost yelled out to Ray, but he held his voice to a whisper. "Let's go," he urged, and went out the door.

Ray lingered a little longer. George, Steve, Jules, and Darren had just slid down the river embankment and out of sight when a couple of soldiers walked around the back corner of the supply building. Ray was just coming out the back door.

The soldiers raised their rifles and yelled for Ray to stop so they could take him prisoner.

Remembering what Darren had just said about being tortured for information about the family, Ray bolted in the opposite direction of the river. If he was going to die, he wanted to help the others escape by leading the soldiers away from them.

The soldiers shot him. They wouldn't be getting any information from him. He was dead.

The soldiers alerted others that there might be more renegades in the area. They searched the town. There were eight soldiers searching along the same alleyway that George, Darren, Jules, and Steve had just come out of.

George, the last in line, saw the soldiers coming. "We will have to find some place to hide quickly," he said.

They were able to put a few streets between themselves and the soldiers.

There were some tanks that had been previously set up at each of the major intersections. Each tank was guarded by a noncommissioned officer and one or more privates who operated it.

Jules noticed one of the tanks. The NCO was leaning against it and smoking a cigarette. It didn't appear he had any idea that renegades were in town.

"Why don't we hide in plain sight and catch a ride home?" Jules said, and nodded toward the tank.

"That could possibly work," said Steve. "I'll walk casually past him. He might think I'm just one of those people allowed back into town. After I get his attention, you guys get him from behind. Be careful."

Steve strolled past the NCO. The man paid absolutely no attention to him. It was as if he had his mind on something else. Steve, thinking fast, said, "Hey, man. Got another cig? I could sure use one."

The soldier took notice of him then. Thinking he might have some friendly conversation, he said, "Sure."

He started to reach in his pocket for his pack of cigarettes. Jules and George grabbed him from behind. The NCO was somehow able to bring up his gun. He fired a shot, and then Darren grabbed the gun.

Jules climbed up on the tank. The NCO had left the hatch open, so when Jules climbed down inside the tank, the private didn't turn around to see who it was. The private started to tell his NCO there had been an alert notifying everyone to be on the lookout for some renegades in the area. He stopped talking when he realized Jules had a rifle aimed directly at his head.

George climbed into the tank next. He turned around to keep his rifle on the NCO as he climbed down into the tank. Steve and Darren climbed into the tank last.

"Dad, you've been shot!" exclaimed Darren.

"I'll be okay. We need to get out of here," said

The End Is Not Yet

Steve.

Darren was about to reach up to close the hatch when they heard some soldiers yell from outside. "Hey, guys. See anything of those renegades we're looking for? We heard a gunshot."

George put the rifle right against the NCO's forehead.

The NCO shouted back, "No. All has been quiet around here. We heard a car backfire just a minute or so ago."

"Well, keep your guard up." The soldiers continued down the street.

After the soldiers left, George traded places with the private. He drove the tank out of town. The other three tied up the private and the NCO with rope they'd taken from the plumbing supply store. They found some tape in the tank and used it to cover the soldiers' mouths.

When they were about five miles from the farm, George pulled the tank off the roadway, drove it into a gully, and stopped.

George stated, "We can make it home from here, even with Steve being hurt."

"Why don't we leave the rest of our food and some water for these guys, just in case it takes a while before they are found?" suggested Jules. "Grandma read me some passages from the Bible that said we should feed our enemy."

They all agreed.

Steve suggested, "Why don't we cut their ropes in half? That would give us time to get away, and still give them half a chance in case they aren't found right away."

The private kept struggling and trying to talk. Darren reluctantly removed the tape. The private poured his heart out. "If you will take us with you, we will fight for you. Your God is our God. Please."

Jules, arguing with his own heart, said, "Do we dare trust them?"

The NCO struggled to talk. They removed his tape. "It's true. We were talking about the real truths of this war. It doesn't match up with what we believe in. When you were going to leave us some food and water…we knew. Please don't leave us for them. They will only kill us anyway, because you got away. Your God really is our God."

The tank was left in the gully with no supplies and no bodies. The group of six travelled the rest of the way on foot, with Steve supported by his two sons.

Steve, George, Darren, and Jules made it back home because of Ray's willingness to give up his life for them. They told everyone at the bunker how Ray had gotten them inside the plumbing supply store, and how he had died so the people in the bunker could live. They introduced their new friends as Noncommissioned Officer Neal Strait and

The End Is Not Yet

Private Olan Snyder, who soon became part of the family.

Steve's wound was not serious. He had bled a lot, but the bullet had gone cleanly through his side and missed any vital organs. As with the wounds the others had received, it just needed to be cleaned and allowed time to heal.

***

Along with the droughts came the locusts. They were migrating all over the world. They would land in an area long enough to strip the fields and damage the crops. They would consume all of the vegetation. Then they would move on to another area.

From a lookout position, a soldier was watching for any signs of danger or renegades. Out of nowhere, in the distance, a shadow advanced toward him. He raised his binoculars to get a better look. In that instant, he no longer needed the binoculars. The shadow was no longer a shadow. Locusts swarmed all over him. Soon he was not there. His bones fell to the earth as if they had never been connected.

This was a new species of migratory locust. It was not like the locusts that covered the earth and ate all of the vegetation. This species fed on vegetation and flesh. When it was in its gregarious phase, it would swarm and feed on anything—plants or animals. When this new species was in its solitude phase, it would search out and use flesh, instead of sand, to plant its eggs in. The warm moisture provided by a living host was perfect for its needs.

**

After being out with the group on a lengthy scavenger hunt, George could not wait to go to bed when he got back to the bunker. As he reached his bed, he fell on it and lay there for a short time before undressing.

Arising from a restless night's sleep, George noticed he had some sort of rash on his left hand. It itched a bit, but he didn't think it was anything to worry about. He figured he had just gotten too close to some poison ivy while out scavenging for food the night before. He shrugged his shoulders and decided to have some breakfast.

At breakfast, Harold happened to notice George's arm. "George, what is that redness on your arm?" said Harold.

George looked down at his arm to see the redness was no longer just on his hand. It had advanced halfway up his arm, toward his elbow. In bewilderment, George responded, "I don't know. I woke up with it like this."

"Are you allergic to anything you might have gotten next to?"

"I don't know. I don't think I'm allergic to anything. I thought that maybe I rubbed my arm against a plant last night when we were out hunting for food. I don't remember being by any strange plants, though."

"Let me put something on it," Harold said. "That redness looks mean. Maybe I can help alleviate any itching or pain."

"I sure would appreciate that. It is itching something fierce right now," George answered.

Harold tried a salve on George's arm, but all it did was make the redness worse. So he carefully washed it off. "Well," said Harold, "let's try just keeping it clean for a few days, and see if it goes away. We'll keep an eye on it."

Harold asked the group if anyone else had similar symptoms. Tasha responded that she didn't have anything like that, but her ear had been feeling funny, and she had been hearing funny noises all morning.

"Let me take a look," Harold offered. He got out a magnifying glass with a flashlight attachment and looked in her ear. With some surprise, he stated, "My, we do have a culprit in there."

He used a long wire with a soft hook on the end to pull a bug out of Tasha's ear. "I haven't seen one for a long time," said Harold, "but this sure looks like a tiny locust. The coloring of yellow and brown, with black markings, would be correct, but I've never seen one with tiny streaks of red before. Of course, I don't know all the species of locust.

Locusts only eat vegetation, though, so everything should be okay. Sue, would you finish up here by helping Tasha with an ear bath, please?"

Sue stated, "I'd be glad to."

She immediately prepared a cleansing solution for Tasha's ear. After Sue finished cleansing Tasha's ear, she told her to make sure to tell them immediately if anything strange started to happen in her ear.

As the days went by, George's arm got worse instead of better. An abundance of tiny bumps rose under his skin. Not knowing exactly what it was, Harold was not sure what to do. He kept praying for a miracle.

It had been about a week. The arm looked worse, but the redness had not advanced any farther up the arm.

To make matters worse, Tasha told them her ear was getting so sore it was hard to keep from crying. Harold examined her ear again and saw that it was starting to swell shut. He would have to figure out something for her soon, or she would have a severe infection, if she hadn't contracted one already.

Little Shari had been listening to the adults talk. She knew that George and Tasha were not feeling very well. She asked her mom for a drink of soda. She wanted to share it with George. Seeing the earnestness in her daughter's eyes, Sue agreed and handed Shari half a glass of soda to take to George, who was sitting in the social room.

Shari was new at carrying things while walking, so she started out carrying it very cautiously. She was so excited to be doing a big-girl deed that the closer she got to George, the faster she tried to walk. Just as she was about to get George's attention to give him the soda, she tripped and spilled it on his left arm.

George gasped at the shock of getting doused with liquid so unexpectedly, but he soon realized what had just transpired. Shari started to cry. George comforted her. "That's okay, Shari. I know you meant well. Look, there are still a couple of swallows in the glass. I would be happy to drink it."

As he raised his arm to finish the soda in the glass, he felt an extreme amount of movement on his arm and hand. The bumps had opened up. Tiny bugs were coming out of the holes. They instantly fell to the floor and died. George gasped and called for Harold.

Hearing the commotion, Harold came running. He realized the locust must have been the culprit for all of this. He poured a little soda on George's hand. It only took a moment or two. The bumps started to open up, and the bugs fell out and died. Harold then requested that Tasha allow him to pour a little in her ear. If it didn't work, she wouldn't be any worse than before. She agreed.

Harold warmed the soda just enough to remove the chill. He poured it in her ear. He held her head so the solution would remain in her ear for a couple of minutes. Then he tilted her head the other way so the soda, and possibly some bugs, would fall out. The bugs came out in a glob. He flushed her ear with soda a second time. When no more bugs came out, he flushed her ear with peroxide and then a saline solution to clean it.

Within the next couple of days, the redness was gone from George's arm, and the swelling was gone from Tasha's ear. Things had returned to normal. The locust incident travelled by word of mouth through the bunkers. It was good information to pass on in case this happened to others.

The news did not just travel through the bunkers. Another man heard of this news. He knew about the trouble the world was having with the locust, so he sent a message to his dear friend in Europe, Anthony Clemenz. If anyone could figure out a way to use this new information to rid the world of the new species of locust, it would be Clemenz.

***

Scorpions followed the locusts.

The scorpions aestivated during the drought. They dug themselves into the ground until the drought eased up. Scorpions made up social colonies with not just one brood of about thirty-five, but multiple broods with numbers ranging in the hundreds of thousands.

The few humans who made it through the drought were oblivious to the presence of the scorpions. The scorpions would come out of their dormant state and lie in wait for the evening to come. If a human crossed their path, a few scorpions would sting the person with enough venom to bring him or her down, while other scorpions would spray acid and start dissolving the flesh. When the person was softened sufficiently, all of the scorpions would move in to suck up their reward.

The scorpions that did not colonize would sting humans separately. None alone had enough venom to bring down a human, but one scorpion could sting and cause pain. Then another scorpion would move in and sting again. This would happen repeatedly. In the end, the victim wished he or she had been stung by the more poisonous scorpions such as the death stalker, rather than endure this torture.

This was only the beginning of the plagues to cross the lands. The people were nervous. The last days were definitely upon them.

Chapter 10

The World Leader Emerged

The drought continued. This caused one-third of the world's vegetation to burn up. The remaining water was slowly giving up sea creatures to an unknown death. Earthquakes and volcanic eruptions were devastating anywhere the droughts were not reaching. Disease, epidemics, and fighting were killing off one-third of the world population. Chaos was everywhere. Nations were fighting against nations. Bombs were being sent back and forth.

Manchu Zhang, the former president of China and chosen leader of the World Council, called an assembly of all the leaders of the countries of the world.

Zhang was a small man in stature, but he was very mean and ruthless. His country had beaten them all in war, so he was naturally the one to lead them. He considered himself the only one capable of leading the world, and he meant to ensure his leadership by dominating everything and everyone.

He opened the assembly by saying, "This will be a new regime. We will be one. With the World Council leading, the people will be happy. If they are not happy, we can secure for them places in the castles of life." He laughed at his sordid joke and expected the others to laugh too. They did so through gritted teeth. They knew that if they angered Zhang, they might end up in the castles of life themselves.

Zhang referred to the prisons as the castles of life. In his mind, it was funny that humans would be used as food for other humans to have life.

Leader Zhang continued, "These have been trying times for all. It is time for the past disagreements to be set aside. You will speak to your people. Tell them all will be better now that we have a World Council. We are all one now, so we must all have the same money. Can you imagine having to carry around yen for this country and dollars for that country? We will make it easier for everyone.

"You will set up your banks to be used as digital stations. There will no longer be any use for money. Tell your people they must turn in all money, silver, and gold, and they can be credited with a total of what they now possess. That way their current possessions will not lose any value.

"We won't tell them, but we will keep two-thirds

of that value. Tell them that a portion will be kept in a fund for emergencies. They don't need to know that we will never let them use that fund. One-third should be enough for them to get by…and to keep them under our rule. After all, once they turn it in to us, what can they do?

"We will put a new system in place. There will be cards they can slide through machines, like in the past, but these cards will document all of their earnings. The machines will automatically approve or reject their purchases. If we deem an item unnecessary, it will be denied by the card. As they deposit their work hours on the cards, there will be an allotment made to their accounts to purchase food and other necessary items.

"We must also have only one religion. If anyone speaks of God, you must ask that person a question: With all of the death and pestilence, where is the promise of His coming?" said Zhang mockingly.

A member raised his hand as if to ask a question. Zhang directed his look toward a guard. "Take that man to the castles of life."

As the guard left with the man, Zhang returned his gaze to the members in front of him. "Does anyone else have a question he would like to interrupt me with?"

He continued, "The wiretaps that have been in place for many years will now be activated. Every call will be monitored. Any attempt at treason, or any talk of God, will be punishable by death.

"Game devices will be reactivated. One game device will be given to each household as a gift. After all, the children must play. The hidden monitors inside the devices will allow us to see inside every home and shelter.

"None will dare defy us!"

World Council Leader Zhang soon ordered the opening of the broadcasting stations. He wanted to speak to all of the people.

"You must not worry about the drought and plagues happening in some of the lands. We will find a way to protect our people," he said.

"The people who have perished in those lands have done so because they chose to believe in their god. Some would have denied believing in this false god, but if they did not believe in him, then why are they dead? See, if you believe in this false god, you will die.

"Our religion is the only religion. Those who are not with us will be sought out by their own deeds. They will fall by the wayside and die, as you have seen.

"Where is the promise of His coming?

"This god of yours does not care about you, or he would come and deliver you out of this.

"You must join our oneness in religion. As there can only be one united world, there can only be one united religion. Anything else is an atrocity. They are leeches that will drain you of your humanity. You must join our league to survive against them. People will come to you, speaking of love and kindness. The true kindness comes from within our union."

The broadcast was played repeatedly. People listened. Some believed what Zhang had said. Others, being made to feel like outcasts, pretended to believe to avoid being singled out and killed. The true love of God was not in their hearts.

***

Troy was doing his normal duties of watching the security cameras and listening to the radio. This time it was not static he was hearing. The radio was working. "Hey, everyone, there's a broadcast coming over the radio! Maybe they will announce all of this is over, and we can go aboveground and live free again."

They turned the radio up so everyone could hear it. As they listened, the hearts of everyone in the Porter bunker sank.

Debbie started to cry. "All those people are dying, and he is using that to get others to follow the World Council. I'm having a hard time fighting off the hatred I have for that man, if that is what he is."

The End Is Not Yet

Debbie sat in the rocking chair. Little Shari came to her and wanted up on her lap. She lifted little Shari up. Debbie picked up the Bible and started to read it. With an innocent child in her lap and the Bible in her hand, soon the feeling of hatred that was making her heart so heavy started to fade.

Others gathered around her and requested she read it aloud.

She started by reading the scriptures that affirmed this would happen. She read, "knowing this first: that scoffers will come in the last days, walking according to their own lusts, and saying, "Where is the promise of His coming? For since the fathers fell asleep, all things continued as *they were* from the beginning of creation."

Debbie strongly urged her family and friends, saying, "Now, more than ever, we need to believe in God and ask forgiveness for our sins. If we keep faith in Him, He will deliver us from all of this. I know He will."

***

The World Council took control of the new temple that had been built at the temple mount in Jerusalem.

Shortly afterward a man came out of Europe. His name was Anthony Clemenz. He was an average man with kind eyes and an intriguing smile. He had an abundance of warmth for the weary people who met him.

He held himself with much dignity and poise. He was quite witty and knowledgeable in the ways of the world. Some tried, but no one was able to catch him off guard. He always took his time to speak, and he said just the right things to rebuke the ones that challenged him. Often he would make his answer into a funny joke or a friendly gesture. Others around him would laugh, and everyone was happy.

People often suggested, "If only he could be the ruler of the world, we would all be better off."

Anthony Clemenz requested a conference with the Council. He said he had recommendations for fixing the world's problems and making everyone love the Council. Naturally the Council decided to give him audience.

Clemenz also requested to speak with Zhang prior to the meeting. He said he had some ideas that were for his ears only. Zhang told him that his ideas had better be good, or he would be sent to the castles of life for wasting his time. Zhang allowed Clemenz to meet with him privately prior to the start of the council meeting.

Clemenz seemed to cast a spell over those he chose to rule. "Leader Zhang, you are the highest of all the elite. If you back what I propose, the rest will follow. They will look upon you alone as their savior in their time of need. You won't have to threaten the people or even command them. They will simply do your bidding.

"Listen to what I propose, and follow my example. I can make you rich beyond belief. All people will bow down before you. You will be the great one."

Zhang didn't know it, but in the short time they talked, Clemenz implanted the idea in his head that he would offer Clemenz to be leader over all.

They entered the meeting room side by side. The council members were in small groups. Some were standing, and some were seated, but all were discussing what this Anthony Clemenz had to offer them.

"Everyone, please be seated and give us your attention," said Zhang. "For those of you who do not know him, I would like to present Anthony Clemenz. He has come to us to discuss how we might ease the pain of the peoples of our world. Give him your ear, for he is very wise."

The members of the council were taken aback by the manner in which Zhang was speaking. They wondered what could have caused this change in character.

Anthony Clemenz looked over the group in the room. *What chumps,* he thought. *I will eat these people for breakfast!*

He began to speak. "As you know, there is much death at our doors. Even some of your family members have passed away due to disease and war. It is time for all this to pass away from you. We will show the people compassion and love for our fellow humans."

No one noticed he was using *we* instead of *you*. He was already taking over.

"First, we will gather the most intelligent members of society. It will not matter from which countries. They will all work together to solve the problems of humankind. The top scientists, botanists, chemists, physicians, and whoever else is needed will be summoned. They will concentrate solely on alleviating the plagues, until they have completed the task.

"We will show all humankind that people are responsible for their own destinies. They will love the Council, and you will be the one they praise. Not some invisible god. Let me be the first to share all my hard work, and show you that I have found the remedy to our locust problem. Kindly watch my demonstration."

He had an assistant bring a see-through plastic container filled with deadly locusts into the room. The container had an opening at one end, where Clemenz connected a hose. Through the hose, he put a small amount of solution into the container. In less than a minute, all of the locusts in the container were dead.

The Council was astounded at the swiftness of

this solution.

"The solution is a mixture of carbonic acid, sodium bicarbonate, and simple syrup. This is a solution used to make carbonated soft drinks. So you see, it works well, and it will not harm humans or animals. It also can be made rather cheaply.

"We will send out planes to spray everywhere. We will supply the people with this spray for free, and they can spray this solution in their own homes. The locusts will not survive, and the people will adore you."

By the time Clemenz finished, his wisdom had captivated everyone. They thought he could do no wrong, and he was clearly the one to lead them.

Mesmerized by Clemenz, Leader Zhang announced, "I relinquish my title as leader of the World Council. I give it over to Anthony Clemenz. He is the *true* leader. He will save us and the world!"

It was done. Anthony Clemenz was now the leader over all.

Anthony Clemenz began immediately to make changes. He stayed true to his word. First he saw to the release of everyone being held in the castles of life. They were allowed to return to their homes, where they could begin working to gather food for themselves and the World Council.

He gathered the most intelligent people to work

on the plagues. The deaths of loved ones from sickness and disease diminished.

He spoke to all nations about loving one another. Soon the fighting and bombing stopped. There was talk of peace everywhere. All of the countries dismantled most of their armies.

The people loved Clemenz for this. He seemed to be the kind, loving savior they had waited for all their lives. They were on the verge of calling him God.

He declared there would no longer be any cards with which to purchase food. He told the people that cards could be lost or stolen. Without the cards they would not be able to purchase necessary items. He had a better system.

In reality, he was going to ensure that no one would be able to pass a card from one person to another. There would be no sharing of points or supplies. He was about to ensure that no one could do anything without his consent, and he would definitely know who the believers in God were. He was about to implement the mark of the beast.

For his new plan, all people had to have a universal number imprinted in their right hand or forehead. That universal number was 666. Every man, woman, and child had to have this mark. Without it, they would not be given food to eat or fuel to keep their homes heated. They would not be given medicine or medical care of any kind. All the necessities of life would be kept from them. They would die, and no one would care.

Three members of the council had been uneasy with Clemenz's appointment. They felt that the leadership was given to him too fast. Just because he knew how to kill the locusts, and promised that the people would love the Council, did not prove that he was the best man to lead the world.

They believed in the World Council, but they loved their country and their people. They had been able to dissuade Zhang from imposing some of his cruelty on their countries, but Clemenz was not Zhang.

They felt this new practice of marking the people, along with some other new rulings from Clemenz, were unusually cruel.

They assumed speaking out in numbers would make a difference to this new leader. He had shown kindness in his dealings with them in the past. They were sure they could get him to understand the error of his thinking. They failed to realize that *he* was the leader now. They were no longer the leaders of anything.

He put up with their arguing for about a month. Then he had had enough of their insolence. He had them tortured and killed. To show his power over their dominions, he had banners displayed throughout all the countries. The banners each contained a dragon and a beast.

He told Zhang the dragon was to honor him for relinquishing the rule of the Council. The beast was to represent the three heads who thought they could rule him with their insolence. The beast was designed using the crests of their countries. The body was like a leopard, the feet were like those of a bear, and the mouth was like the mouth of a lion. No one in those lands, or any other place, would dare challenge Clemenz again.

With every change Clemenz made, his looks became increasingly sinister. He no longer had a look of kindness and gentleness. He didn't give off a feeling of warmth. He was starting to show his true self. His eyes became beady little holes in his face. His eyebrows had ridged tightly, as if he was continually scowling, and were pointy in the center. His face became gruesome and wrinkled. His hands and feet looked like claws.

One evening in the courtyard of the World Council building, Clemenz called for a gathering of the people. He wanted to demonstrate his true powers. He ordered this demonstration to be aired on all television stations and radio bands. He stood on a podium so that everyone would have a good view of his demonstration.

He had a horse led out in front of the crowd. With a wave of his hand, the horse sat on its haunches, rolled over, and played dead.

A man from the crowd yelled out, "Any dumb

animal can be made to do tricks!" He laughed loudly, and the crowd began to laugh too.

This was exactly what Anthony Clemenz wanted. He peered at the laughing man. The man was lifted in the air and floated toward Anthony Clemenz. He was then released from this hold and dropped before Anthony's feet.

The man's face and body were dripping with sweat caused by his fear. He had laughed at Clemenz, and now he dreaded the price he would have to pay.

"Why are you afraid of me? Are you not the one that scoffed and laughed?" asked Anthony.

"I fear what you will do to me," the man responded, and he cowered close to the ground.

Anthony slyly stated, "I like a man who is not afraid to laugh at what he thinks is funny. Let me show you my gratitude."

Again Anthony Clemenz peered at a spot in front of the crowd.

A table appeared. It was set for someone to dine. In the center of the table was a small vase with a single flower in it. There was a crystal goblet for water, and one for wine. A metal cloche covered a plate that was nestled on a placemat. This was all set atop a crisp, clean tablecloth.

Clemenz prompted the man to sit at the table. The man slowly moved toward it. He hesitantly sat in the chair provided.

With a motion of his hand, Anthony Clemenz caused the cloche to rise.

"What do you see on the plate?" he inquired of the man.

"Oh! There is a beautifully roasted rabbit with a huge portion of fresh, steamed vegetables, and a side of a delicious-looking fruit salad." The man salivated. "I did not know there was any food like this available anymore."

"Are these not your favorite foods?" Anthony asked.

The man answered, "Oh, yes. These are definitely my very favorite things to eat."

The crowd gasped and gagged. They could see what was really on the plate. There was a dead, rotting rat that still had its fur and guts hanging from its belly. There were clumps of horse manure placed in a pile next to the rat, and in a smaller dish was an assortment of eyeballs.

Anthony Clemenz encouraged the man. "Go ahead. Indulge in the wonderful plate of food. Show everyone your reward for laughing and scoffing at what you think is funny!"

The man ate as if he had never eaten before. He gorged himself so fast that the hair of the rat still hung around his lips when he finished.

The End Is Not Yet

With the last bite, Anthony Clemenz allowed him to see what he was really about to put in his mouth. It was a portion of the rat's head.

The man felt the hair around his mouth and started to vomit.

Clemenz was tired of the game. "You dare vomit up the food I have given you to eat? You are ungrateful. You can be no longer."

He caused the man to rise in the air again, and with a simple snap of his fingers, the man was set on fire and was gone.

Clemenz, however, still heard mocking from the crowd. He heard whispers that it was just a mass hallucinatory trick.

To further demonstrate his supernatural powers, Clemenz summoned Manchu Zhang to step forward on the podium. He ordered him to be killed. A soldier stepped forward and drew his saber.

Zhang pleaded, "Please, sir, what have I done to deserve this? Tell me, and I will make it right. Do not kill me. I have been your most loyal supporter."

Clemenz motioned for the soldier to stop.

"You have been my most trusted follower," said Clemenz. "You believe in me, don't you? Then why do you not trust me now? I will show you mercy."

Ignoring any further pleadings from Zhang,

Clemenz motioned for the soldier to continue with his deed. The soldier stabbed Zhang through the heart, and Zhang fell dead on the podium.

"Now you will see what true mercy is," said Clemenz. "You will also know if this is a hallucination or not."

Clemenz pointed at the dead body at his feet. Zhang sat up, and then he stood. He was alive and well.

Zhang knelt before Clemenz. He reached out for his hand, and he kissed it. "You are the true God," said Zhang.

The crowd fell to their knees, but Clemenz had not forgotten that the entire crowd had laughed with the scoffing man. Clemenz knew the demonstration would happen that way. He had prepared for it, and he was not about to let it go unpunished.

Before the decline of the scorpion plague, Clemenz had ordered some of the scorpions to be saved for future study and use. He had had some of the scorpions brought to the courtyard earlier that day. Clemenz had them let loose, knowing they would go into hiding until evening. He knew they would lie in wait until they could approach and sting their victims.

He had planned the demonstration just right. Just as he brought Zhang back to life, a man in the crowd screamed, "I...I've been stung by a scorpion!"

As the crowd looked around them, they could see hundreds of scorpions running among them. People were being stung, and they were screaming and crying. People yelled throughout the crowd, "The scorpion plague is back!"

Above the screams of the crowd, they could hear Anthony Clemenz's laughter. "Now you have seen my powers," he said. "Do not mock me!"

Clemenz soon gathered an army of two hundred men to show the world he was the almighty one to follow. Anyone that stood in the army's way was killed. To show his strength and ability, Clemenz armed his soldiers with unusual, previously unseen weapons. He said these weapons were his magic. All who followed him would be safe.

He professed to the people, "I am God! You must follow me to save yourselves. Without my leadership, each person will be alone. Man will turn against wife; parents will no longer care about their children. Brothers will turn against brothers. But I can save you from all of that. I am God!"

He was now the full image of Satan, but his deception and evilness blinded the people. They loved him, so they could not see the truth. No matter what he did, if he told the people it was for their good, they believed him. They unquestioningly accepted the idea that he was God.

Chapter 11

'Tis Written

Some continued to believe in the real God. They continued to pray and seek forgiveness for their sins.

It was written that the Lord God would give power to his "two witnesses to prophesy for one thousand, two hundred and sixty days, clothed in sackcloth". They would have "power to shut heaven, so that no rain falls in the days of their prophecy; and they have power over waters to turn them into blood, and to strike the earth with all plagues, as much as they desire."

Those who loved the Lord knew that all these things must come to pass. They prayed for the will of God to be done. They knew that the Scripture said the witnesses would be clothed in sackcloth, so that meant they would appear as common people. They would not be rich or overly endowed with possessions.

Two such men roamed among the people. To all they met, they preached the Word of God from the Holy Scriptures.

Some believed, and allowed themselves to be baptized. Others turned their backs on the witnesses. They said, "We know the real God. He is at the new temple. He will save us. As to your god, where is the promise of his coming? Our God has supernatural powers. He has shown this to us. What has your god shown? Your believers die with disease and famine."

The scoffers turned away from the witnesses and went straight to the new temple to tell Clemenz about the enemies lurking in the land.

Anthony Clemenz sent his army to find the two that prophesized and witnessed for their god. The army found the witnesses and brought them before him.

"So you are the ones who mock me. Do you know what I can do to you? Maybe you missed my demonstration. Shall I give you a special demonstration?" With that, Anthony Clemenz made a motion. A ball of fire fell from the sky and landed in the courtyard.

The witnesses looked at Anthony. One of them spoke:

"Yes, you could have us killed. You can torture us

or try to tempt us, but in the end we will be dead. Being dead, however, we would ultimately be with our Lord God."

The love the witnesses held for their Lord God so angered Anthony Clemenz that he had them tortured and killed. He ordered their bodies not to be buried. The bodies would be left to lie in the streets for all to see. He wanted everyone to witness what the false god allowed to happen to his followers.

He declared it to be a holiday. The people rejoiced and partied. They sent gifts to each other in celebration of the death of the two witnesses who had brought such misery and torment. After three and a half days, the witnesses who had lain dead in the streets stood on their feet.

Everyone who saw them became frightened. They cowered in fear. They didn't know if they should believe what their eyes were seeing. They were sure that Anthony Clemenz had made this happen. They remembered the scorpions in the courtyard. They were sure that they would be punished for something, although they didn't know what it was. He had ordered it to be a holiday, and they were celebrating his greatness.

The witnesses heard a loud voice from heaven saying to them, "Come up here," and the witnesses ascended into heaven. All enemies of the witnesses watched as the witnesses ascended and were carried up to heaven on a cloud.

At that same moment, a great earthquake struck the city. Thousands were killed. The rest were afraid, knowing the Lord God had caused this to happen. They praised the Lord God in heaven.

This angered Anthony Clemenz, so he sent his army to find all the followers of these two witnesses and their god. Mercilessly the army went forth on a murderous rampage. The persecution of the true believers continued all over the world. The world leader's army dropped bombs on any city thought to hold people that believed in any god other than Anthony Clemenz.

The people who lived in those cities became vigilantes and took up arms. They went through the streets asking people if they believed in the lord god or the real God. If someone showed the slightest hesitation in answering, the vigilantes shot them. Then they sought out their families and killed them too. Their bodies were left to rot in the streets as if in mockery of the witnesses.

The vigilantes hoped this would make Clemenz see how much they loved him, and how sorry they were to have doubted him. Hopefully he would show them mercy and make his army leave their cities alone.

The army continued its mission. It shot five-megaton warheads from submarines along all coastal ports. The disaster was horrific. The flesh of the people melted away from their bones. Their eyes melted out of their sockets. Half of the world's population was annihilated.

Anthony Clemenz had the prisons reopened, and he threw the believers in them. He could then torture them at his whim.

Hailstorms started. Fifty-pound hailstones were hurled onto the earth. Earthquakes were happening in all parts of the world. Many people, including those in the army, sought refuge in mountain caves to avoid the hailstones and to hide from the ash and fumes from the earthquakes.

Hiding did not help. The air was not breathable. Many perished. Many wished they could die, but they did not die.

Those living in properly built bunkers, and who so loved the Lord God, were spared from those catastrophes.

***

Meanwhile, at the Smith bunker, Justin Smith and Ted Lentner were becoming very close friends.

Theodore Lentner was a young man who had been rescued from the encampment. He was close in age to Justin, and they shared the same tastes in music, games, and ideas about the future.

Ted never found his mother after they were split up at the encampment, and Ted's father had been beheaded before his very eyes. This left a scar on his heart. He kept his secret well, but the grief was more than he could bear. Soon he found himself releasing his anxieties by discussing his hateful thoughts with Justin.

Alone, neither young man would have come up with a plan to get back at the soldiers and Anthony Clemenz, but together they were like two totally different people and came up with many ideas.

Justin told Ted about the adventure, as he called it, with Paul Johnson. He said how proud he was to have been part of it, when Paul made himself into a human grenade.

The more they talked, the more they thought it was their duty to avenge the deaths of Ted's parents and Justin's brother, Clark.

Justin had forgotten all about his talk with Tabler after Paul's death. He also figured he was old enough to make his own decisions. He didn't need his older brother telling him what to do.

Ted and Justin made plans to go out in the daytime so they could see where the traps were located. They didn't want to get caught in one and have their plans ruined before they got started. They decided to use the excuse that they were taking some garbage out to bury it.

The next morning after breakfast, they set the stage by offering to take care of the garbage. They bagged some rifles and ammunition to look like part of the garbage, and out they went.

Their plan worked perfectly. They were outside the bunker, but instead of burying the garbage, they stashed it in some brush that grew between a couple of trees. They figured the faster they got away from the bunker, the less likely they would be found by anyone from the bunker who decided to go looking for them when they realized they were gone.

They travelled for a couple of hours. They were close to some of the generator traps when they heard the helicopters coming. The pair hid in the woods and hoped the helicopters wouldn't be able to find them. The helicopters were equipped with special heat-sensing equipment. The equipment could give readings in day or night.

When the helicopters started shooting, Justin decided to use himself as a decoy. He wasn't aware of any sensory equipment that would allow the men in the chopper to know there were two of them.

"I'm going to run out into that opening to draw their attention," said Justin. "You stay low until they come after me. Then you head back to the bunker."

"But they'll kill you. I won't let you do that," argued Ted.

Ted was a little late with his argument. Justin was already running into the clearing. He waved his arms as if to surrender.

The End Is Not Yet

The helicopter continued to shoot into the trees.

One bullet hit Ted in the leg, and he fell into the mudhole dug to trap soldiers.

Ted was lucky in two ways. First, when he fell into the hole, he was completely submerged in the mud. The coldness of the mud caused a quick drop in temperature in Ted's body. This caused the helicopter sensor to register that the person in the woods had been fatally hit. Second, the generator was not turned on, so he could use the low-hanging branches to pull himself free without being electrocuted.

Ted was able to pull himself out of the mudhole just in time to see Justin being hit with the butt of a rifle and then dragged into the helicopter.

It took a long time, but Ted managed to hobble his way back to the bunker, and to what he thought was safety.

The soldiers in the helicopter notified their ground unit about a dead body in the woods. The ground unit searched for the body, to no avail. Instead, they found Ted's tracks. They followed the tracks for a while, but it was getting late, so they decided to set up camp for the night.

One of the privates went behind two trees to relieve himself. When he got back to his camp, he informed his commanding officer he had found a pile of bagged garbage. The bags didn't show any animal damage or discoloration from the elements, so the people who dumped it had to be close.

The new information gave the commanding officer reason to start the soldiers searching again. When they found what looked like an entrance to a bunker, he had them look for an opening or a latch. The soldiers crisscrossed every inch of the ground. Some were searching east, and others were searching west, in case a latch could only be seen from one direction. In so doing, they tripped the beam that made the door of the bunker open.

***

Justin Smith was brought before Anthony Clemenz and forced down on his knees.

"Who is this that does not freely kneel to me? Are you foolish, or are you one of those lord god followers?" demanded Clemenz mockingly.

Justin fought back. "I am neither. I am not foolish." Knowing his fate if he said he believed in God, he continued, "And how could I believe in one who would allow so many to be punished and die?"

"Sounds as if you are trying to outsmart me. Do you always answer a question with a question?" said Clemenz. He barked an order to his guards. "Take him to the prison. Each night we will put him in the scorpion pens. We will see if he will truly deny his god."

Each night, as dusk set in, the prisoners were brought out of their prison cells and placed in the scorpion pens. The scorpion pens were individual wire cages about the size of coffins. Each prisoner's hands were bound and chained to the top of the pen. This way he or she could not lash out at the scorpions.

The pens were then placed in the prone position. The prisoners could kick at the scorpions, but the pens were so small and tight that they couldn't stop the scorpions from stinging them.

The scorpions came out of hiding and travelled between the wires to their bound and waiting victims. They would sting the prisoners repeatedly until the dawn broke. Then the scorpions would go back to their hiding places until the next dusk came.

Many of the prisoners were broken souls. They knew Clemenz was not God, but they weren't sure what they could do about it. They were prisoners without much hope for living. They knew they would never see the outer world again.

On the third day, the prisoner in the cell across the hallway heard Justin crying. It was not a pained cry. It was more of a mournful cry.

He asked Justin, "What are you doing?"

Justin answered him sorrowfully. "I have sinned against God. I tried to deny Him before Anthony Clemenz. Clemenz knew I was not saying what my true thoughts were, but God also knew my true thoughts. I was neither hot nor cold for the Lord, and now I am suffering.

"I remember the Bible readings that said if I repented and remained faithful unto death, the Lord would give me the crown of life. 'He who overcomes will not be hurt by the second death.' I need to trust in God now. I have been asking for forgiveness of my sins. Now I need to stay faithful. I know they are going to kill me no matter what I do. I don't want to suffer in hell. I know they will lie to me to get me to deny God. I hope I am brave enough not to give into their temptations and attempts to get me to give up my God.

"My brother was right when he tried to keep me from my vengeful ways. I have so much to ask forgiveness for."

The fellow prisoner stated, "I have done so much sinning in my lifetime. I have stolen things. I have raped women. I have even murdered. I have never believed in anything, much less God. I was more than willing to accept the works of Anthony Clemenz, and still I have ended up in here. There is no hope for me. The real God will never look in my direction."

Justin, understanding the man's pain, told him, "It is written that 'for all have sinned and fall short of the glory of God.' Repent your sins. He will know if it comes from your heart or not. If you truly mean it, there will be room for you in heaven."

Soon Justin could hear mournful cries coming

from the cell across the hallway.

On the fourth night, as Justin lay in the scorpion pen, he noticed the soldiers escorting some new prisoners through a glassed-in hallway to the prison cells.

He had to strain his eyes to see who was being escorted. They looked strangely familiar. As they passed near some lights, he could see them very well. It was his family and some of the others who lived in his bunker. They had been taken captive, and now they were here. Ted was not with them.

He wondered if Ted had been caught and tortured until he gave up the location of the bunker. He argued with himself that Ted would never do that. He would never trade all of their lives for his.

Then Justin remembered the garbage that he and Ted hadn't buried. Were his family and friends taken hostage because they had neglected to bury that garbage? Were they both to blame for his family and friends being found and captured? If so, where was Ted?

The evenings in the scorpion pens continued until the tenth day. Something seemed different that night. The scorpions weren't coming out. Then Justin saw why. A huge scorpion was moving toward him.

He thought it looked like the death stalker scorpion he had studied about in school. Death stalker scorpions were only supposed to grow to between three and a half and four and a half inches long. This one was at least seven inches long. It really didn't matter what type of scorpion this was, or how big it was. Justin knew it would be the last scorpion that would ever sting him. The other scorpion stings had so weakened his body that it wouldn't take much to kill him. It was his turn to die. He started to pray.

***

"You know, it has been a while since we have had any contact with the other bunkers. I've been wondering how they are all doing. I am the only doctor between all three bunkers. Would anyone have any objections to my going over to make sure everything is okay?" asked Harold.

Brad agreed. "No objection at all. I've been wondering how they are doing, too. I'd like to go check on them with you."

"I'd like to go too," said Steve.

"Let's go out tonight," suggested Harold.

After dinner, Harold grabbed some medical supplies and his bag. Steve and Brad took up the weapons and ammunition. They set out to visit the Smiths' and Wilkins' bunkers.

"The Smiths' bunker is closer. Let's go that way first," suggested Brad.

As they were getting closer to the Smiths'

bunker, they saw birds feeding. At first it was hard to see what they were all eating. Then they realized what they were seeing under the birds were human bones.

Steve was the first to see Ted Lentner. He moved beside a tree, trying to hide that he was going to vomit.

Ted's body was pecked over, except for his face. He was dead, but the muscles in his face had not relaxed from the anguishing look of pain. It was as if his face was frozen in place.

As they went further, they started to recognize more and more people who had taken up residence in the bunker.

"What could have happened?" Harold asked. "Most of these people would not have been outside on their own. They wouldn't have been able to help with any fighting or defense. They could hardly help themselves."

When they arrived at the bunker, they realized what had happened. "Somehow the soldiers found the bunker and figured out how to open it," Brad said. "They seem to have taken or killed everyone. The ones lying out there are the ones who would have slowed the soldiers down. I assume they killed them and left their bodies for the animals and birds to feed on."

"I didn't see Cliff, Tabler, Justin, or some of the others. I wonder if they got away," Steve said.

Brad answered, "I doubt they got away. If they had, those bodies wouldn't be lying there. Even if they went after the soldiers, they would have taken the time to show their respect and compassion by burying the bodies of their friends first."

Brad continued, "There's really nothing more we can do, so let's go see if the Wilkins' bunker is okay."

They arrived at the Wilkins' bunker a few hours later.

Brad told Fred about what had happened to their friends. All of them bowed their heads in silence. Hearing about what happened was more than anyone could bear. No one wanted to talk after that.

Harold gave Fred the medical supplies he had brought along in case of an emergency. He knew the Wilkins' bunker was not as well stocked medically as the Porters' bunker, so this was his attempt at sharing. He advised them they could count on him for help if the need ever arose.

Finding everyone in good health and telling them the news about the Smiths, Harold, Brad, and Steve decided they'd better head back to their home in case the soldiers were aware of their bunker's location and would decide to go there next.

When they arrived at their home bunker, they were bombarded with questions about how everyone was.

The End Is Not Yet

Harold started to respond to their questions. "The folks at Fred's bunker seem to be doing okay. They will let us know if they ever need anything. The people in the Smiths' bunker..." He almost choked on his words. "They won't be needing any help from us." He couldn't continue, and he hung his head.

Brad spoke softly. "The soldiers have either killed or taken them. There's nothing we can do to help them now. The bunker was completely emptied out."

Steve remained silent. There was nothing more to be said. He didn't want the rest of them to know about the horrible sight of the bodies lying outside for the animals and birds to eat.

Sue said, "I know you probably don't feel like it, but your travels have been long and hard. Would you like something to eat? You all really need to keep your nourishment up."

They agreed they would try to eat something, so the ladies set out to make a light meal. During the hustle of putting the meal together, no one said a word.

Some of the younger kids became rowdy in response to boredom and because they sensed the adults' unrest. Troy decided that now would be a good time to help keep the children quiet. He gathered the children into the social bunker.

When he went to the bookshelves, he found a

few fairy tales and the children's Bible stories his mom had placed there when they first moved into the bunker. When he asked the children which book he should read, they all agreed they wanted to hear the story of baby Jesus.

Troy started a new tradition in the bunker that night. From then on, every night, after the children had eaten their supper, they would ask him to read to them. Troy would do so gladly. It didn't matter which book he read first; they always wanted to hear about baby Jesus at the end. Then they would go to bed without fussing. That was a promise they had made to Troy if he read to them.

After the children were all settled in their beds, the adults were glad to have a little quiet time before they retired for the night. Brad and George sat in the chairs in the social room.

Sasha, the cat, knowing things were getting quieter, curled up on the back of the chair in front of the bookshelves. Three of the dogs curled up on the rug. Kaiser, the fourth dog, wasn't ready to settle down. He got a rubber toy. He carried it over to Brad's feet and dropped it.

Brad looked at the toy and gazed into his dog's eyes. He knew what Kaiser wanted. The dogs had normally played in the soundproof room. There wasn't anything in that room to stop them from running, fetching, and having fun. Without thinking, Brad picked up the rubber toy and gave it a toss. Kaiser took a casual leap and caught it. He carried the toy over to George and dropped it. George, too, picked up the toy and gave it a toss. Soon the other dogs were playing and catching it also.

Then the toy was tossed a little too high. Kaiser jumped for it, but he missed. The toy bounced off his nose and hit Sasha, startling her out of her sleep. She leaped up and away from the object. In so doing, she pushed her feet out to stop herself from hitting the shelves behind her. She accidentally brushed Tasha's vase.

Hearing the commotion, Tasha left the table area and entered the social area just in time to watch her vase turn on the shelf. It was as if the hands of time had slowed down. The vase fell to the floor. It broke into tiny pieces. Tasha's heart sank. Her mouth dropped. A tear started to swell in her eye. She shrieked, but then she quickly covered her hand over her mouth. She swallowed hard, but it was not for the vase. She was remembering having watched the soldiers throw her mother's family heirlooms out the window.

Debbie went to Tasha. She softly placed her arms around her daughter. "The vase is a material item. Hope and faith come from the heart and the love of God. That vase was only a reminder of that hope and love. They are still there, in your heart, where they have always been."

Tasha slowly pulled away from her mother. "Let me get the broom and dustpan. It will help me if I clean up this mess by myself."

Tasha grabbed the broom and dustpan and carefully cleaned up the mess. She made sure she cleaned up every piece so no one could step on it later. She never spoke a word during the time it took her to clean up the vase.

After she bagged up the broken pieces and put the broom and dustpan away, she went to Brad and gave him a daughterly hug. Then she turned to George and gave him a kiss and a hug. She spoke to both of them: "It was only a vase. Everyone here is alive and safe. Because of that, we know there is always hope. Let's be thankful for that."

By the look on her face, everyone could tell she was okay with what happened. She yawned, stretched her arms in the air, and said, "I'm tired. I think I'll go to bed now."

Tasha exited to her sleeping area. George yawned and said, "I think I'll go too." and followed her. Soon the entire bunker was in bed and fast asleep.

Chapter 12

Fresh Meat

Troy Porter had grown into quite an astounding young man. He had finally gained some height. He had broad shoulders and a firm physique. Having weight-lifting equipment and not much else to do might have had something to do with that.

Billy Jordan, on the other hand, was not given the same gifts as Troy. He was taller than Troy, but one couldn't find anyone thinner. He made a scarecrow look fat. As much as he tried to develop muscles, it was of no use. Maybe it was the lack of real protein that kept him from developing properly. Maybe it was from being held captive in the encampment too long.

None of that mattered to these two young men, though. They were best friends. If one couldn't come up with a prank for laughs, the other one could. They were the real souls who kept the bunker laughing.

This early morning, however, they were plotting something quite different.

They had seen a deer on the outdoor camera monitors. The bunker had been on canned and freeze-dried meat for a long time. The droughts had made wild animals almost nonexistent. Fresh meat was unavailable.

They had not been allowed to go out with any groups because of the dangers involved if they ran into soldiers. They were just reaching manhood. Their families didn't want to see that snuffed out. So they were the ones responsible for monitoring the cameras.

They were not thinking about the real danger this might bring upon the bunker if something went wrong. They were young and had it in their minds to give the bunker a nice Sunday-morning surprise.

"Billy, I know it's been a while since I shot a rifle, but my eyesight is good, and I remember everything I was taught. Do you think we should treat the families to some real meat? I know I can kill it. I was always a really good shot. A natural, you might say."

"Knowing you, Troy, I'm sure you could kill it. But no one has been outside for a long time. The radio broadcasts are making everyone use extreme caution. Maybe we should just let well enough alone," suggested Billy.

"I tell you what. We'll go outside and see if that deer is still around. If not, we'll follow its tracks for just a little while. We won't go far. We'll be back with that deer before the others even know we're gone," Troy said. "Wouldn't real meat taste good? We haven't had any in so long. I've almost forgotten what it tastes like."

"Well, okay, but we won't go far, and if we don't see it out there, we come right back. You know, we are supposed to be monitoring those cameras," Billy said.

Troy joked, "We'll still be monitoring the cameras. We'll just be doing it from outside."

They gathered two rifles and some ammunition and snuck out of the bunker. They left the door unlatched so they would be able to sneak back in when they got back. They snuck around the back of the old barn and tried to find the deer. The deer was gone, but they could still see the tracks. They followed the tracks through the woods and over a knoll.

Their stomachs turned sour. They both started to vomit. They never could have imagined the horror before their eyes. The woods around their bunker had been spared from all the gruesomeness they were now witnessing.

The others who had gone out the last time didn't

talk much when they came back. Now Troy and Billy knew why.

There were skeletons everywhere. There was dried blood coagulated over everything. There were remains of animals and humans still being picked at by birds.

"Troy, I don't feel so good anymore. Let's go back to the bunker."

Troy agreed. With reverence, he softly said, "How that one deer survived through all of this, only heaven knows. It is not for us to take its life. We'll head back."

***

Brad and Debbie arose before everyone else in the bunker. Debbie donned her robe and headed for the cooking area to get started on breakfast. Brad had gone to the restroom and then back to their sleeping area to get dressed.

Debbie noticed the bunker door was unlatched, so she latched it and decided to do a walk-through to see who was missing from the bunker. It didn't take her long to see that Troy was not in the surveillance room where he should have been. She then checked to see if Billy was in the bunker. He was not to be found. That figured. Where Troy was, Billy was.

When Brad came into the cooking area, Debbie told him she had found the door unlatched and the boys gone.

"Well, they are probably just outside somewhere close. I'll go take a look and be right back," stated Brad.

Brad stepped outside. He looked around for a while. He couldn't see them. He went back in the bunker to let Debbie know he was going to take a longer look outside.

"We'll let the rest sleep. I'll go with you." Debbie said. She continued to talk as she went to their sleeping area to get dressed. "This is probably all innocent curiosity. Besides, I haven't been outside since we came down here. I'd like the chance to get out for a little while."

Brad said, "We'll have to take the rifles. It's been a long time since you have shot any weapons. Do you think you can still do it?"

Debbie's answer surprised him. "Not only do I think I can still shoot; I know I still can. When some of you have gone out of the bunker for different reasons, those of us left in here did target practice in that farthest bunker. We thought it would be best to keep our skills sharp just in case something came up, and I see it has."

"Okay, let's go," remarked Brad.

They snatched up the rifles, grabbed some ammunition, and headed out to find the boys. They were searching blindly. They did not see any signs to show them the way the boys had gone. They kept walking, hoping they would run into them or find signs that would lead to them.

They heard someone talking, but they could tell it was not Troy or Billy. They decided to sneak closer to make sure that whoever it was did not have the boys. They got close enough to see it was a group of soldiers. Brad and Debbie decided to hide in the brush until it was safe to move again.

The soldiers' attention seemed fixed on something just a short distance to the right of where Brad and Debbie were hiding.

Tom Sinclair was a private in the US Army. He was a true American who loved his country. He hated what the World Council was doing to the people of America, but there was nothing he could do about it. He had enlisted in the army about six months before the war started. He had to follow orders. His life, and the lives of everyone in his family, depended on it.

Anthony Clemenz had supposedly dismantled all of the armies except for his own, but certain countries were allowed to retain a few military units for the sake of seeking out those who might retaliate against Clemenz. The soldiers weren't asked if they wanted to stay in the army. They were selected. Refusal meant death.

Tom was trying to stay loyal to the service of his country's government, hoping that one day it would change back from a world order to individual countries. Secretly, he was trying to stay even more loyal to his country's people, and to God.

Whenever food came, Tom refused to take any meat. He was not about to eat the flesh of his fellow humans. He knew someday he would have to make a stand for what he truly believed in.

Peter was a close buddy of Tom's. They stayed near each other on missions. They covered each other's back. During private talks, they realized they felt the same way about a lot of issues. They didn't trust Clemenz. They didn't trust the meat. They believed in God.

Tom, Peter, and a few other soldiers were out on a reconnaissance mission.

Tom saw it first. To the others around him, he whispered, "Hey, keep quiet. Do you see what I see?"

"Oh, yeah. I see it," whispered Peter.

The others around them were not used to hunting, and they couldn't distinguish what Peter and Tom were talking about or what they were looking at. Just then, the deer made a slight move.

"Hey, there it is!" remarked another soldier, a little too loudly. The deer was alerted and darted away. In an anxious frenzy, a soldier raised his rifle and shot wildly at the deer. He missed.

Peter snapped at the soldier, "What'd ya do that

for? We could have finally eaten some meat."

Tom said to Peter, "I guess we're back to rice, spuds, and beans."

The other soldier said, "You guys are weird. You don't eat meat anyway. What's wrong with you?"

"What's wrong with *you*?" Tom said. "How can you eat human flesh? You could be eating your own cousin for all you know, but you don't even care."

"Since Anthony Clemenz took over, no one is eating human meat anymore. He put a stop to all that, or hadn't you heard?" scoffed the soldier.

"Well, you can believe that if you want to," Tom said. "As for me, I'll go on eating the things I'm sure of. I don't trust that Clemenz."

Still hiding in the bushes, Brad whispered, "It appears they are still eating humans. I wish we could help these two young men. It seems they don't want to be a part of Clemenz's—or anybody else's—army."

"I wish we could too. Even now. With all the changes in the army, all soldiers aren't bad. Some still love their fellow humans," said Debbie.

In the clearing, the soldier continued the argument. "If I didn't know better, I would think you two were renegade lovers, and believers in that false god. Are you? Would you rather starve than eat the flesh of humans?"

The End Is Not Yet

The soldier gave them an odd, leering look and moved over by the rest of the men. They whispered a few things back and forth among themselves, as if in a football huddle.

"I think we need to take care of these two," suggested the soldier.

"And how shall we go about doing that? You know we'll be brought up on charges for murder," remarked one of his buddies.

"They won't bring us up on charges. When we tell them why we shot these two lowlifes, they'll give us medals. Clemenz will have us promoted into his special army. We just need to stick together with our story," said the first soldier.

A few minutes later, the other soldiers lifted their rifles and aimed them at Tom and Peter as if they were a firing squad.

When the others had gone off into a group, Tom and Peter had walked over by a tree to talk privately.

Peter looked at Tom with worry in his eyes. "Something doesn't feel right. I know we just had a confrontation with that guy, but I have a gut feeling this is not over. I wonder if we will make it back to the rest of the unit to tell our side of this argument."

Tom was worried too, but he didn't want to sound like it. "I'm sure it's over. You're just feeling the bad vibes still hanging in the air. They wouldn't do anything to us. They know they'd be brought up on charges. These days, that doesn't mean a court-martial. That means death—"

Tom had not finished his sentence when they sensed movement. They turned toward their fellow soldiers. Their eyes widened and their mouths dropped open.

The soldiers fired and executed Tom and Peter.

Debbie jerked. An almost inaudible sound escaped her lips. She had been hit by one of the bullets meant for Tom and Peter.

Brad caught her as she fell back, and he gently laid her on the ground. "Let me see how bad it is, Debbie."

Debbie sighed. "No, Brad. It will be over for me soon. In my past, I was neither on fire for the Lord, nor was I cold against him. I feared I would not be worthy to see the New World, but you can, dear. You can help the rest make it. Help them to keep their faith strong for the Lord. Don't let Clemenz win.

"I would rather you lay my body out in the fields as food for the birds and animals. They don't have much else to eat. Please do this for me. It is only my body and not my soul they will eat.

"I love…" Her words faded away as she drifted into death.

The End Is Not Yet

Brad held her, rocking her for a long time, whispering, "Debbie don't go. Don't go." He cried until his tears seem to dry up in his eyes.

Brad did as she requested. After the soldiers left the area, he carried her body into the field to be eaten by the scavengers. He then headed back to the bunker to see if the boys had returned.

When he arrived they still had not yet returned.

***

The boys were getting close to the old barn when they heard some talking in front of them. They were in trouble. They would have to go in that direction to get back to the bunker. They crouched by a tree, trying to discern what the people were saying. Maybe they knew them, but the boys wanted to make sure before they went any further.

They had no such luck. The voices belonged to soldiers.

It was a small group of soldiers. They thought they could impress Anthony Clemenz if they found and killed those so-called god-fearing people.

"Oh God, we could sure use Your help now," the boys whispered.

They decided to circumvent the area. Maybe they could get around to the other side of the barn and sneak in through some of the loose boards in the far side.

They were able to sneak a little closer to the barn. They were almost there. They had just a few more yards to go.

Suddenly Billy felt a sting in his leg. A snake had bitten him. It was a strange snake. The boys had not seen any that looked like that in this part of the country.

Troy used the butt of his rifle to kill it. Troy decided he should probably take it back to the bunker in case someone there knew what kind of snake it was. Maybe it would help Harold know what to do to help Billy if he could see what the snake looked like.

The snake almost bit right into the bone.

Troy found some light branches and tore his T-shirt bottom to make a splint for Billy's leg. He hoisted Billy on his back and started working his way around to the far side of the barn. The only thing he could think of was to get Billy back by Harold as soon as he could.

A soldier had just finished relieving himself beside one on the trees. He turned around just in time to see Troy and Billy before they had a chance to get out of sight.

Troy did not want to shoot. That might alert the other soldiers. Troy set Billy on the ground as he prepared to counter whatever the soldier was about to do.

The End Is Not Yet

The soldier started to laugh when he saw the age of his opponent. He knew this young lad must have been in the bunkers since he was small. The soldier surmised this boy couldn't possibly know how to shoot his rifle, much less know how to fight a soldier.

All of the Philbig boys had taken Tang Soo Do classes when they were little. Steve and Tonja thought they should know how to protect themselves in case of an emergency.

"You can't be too careful, with the way this world is going," Steve had said.

The soldier charged at Troy.

Troy automatically went into self-defense mode. He snapped his left leg up and out straight while pirouetting. He connected with the soldier right in the head, knocking him off his feet.

The soldier barely hit the ground, and he was back up again, making another charge at Troy. Troy moved to the side and brought his arm up and behind the soldier. He connected with the soldier's spine.

The soldier was getting tired of this. With his third lunge, he plunged straight into Troy's midsection, forcing him to the ground. He was on top of Troy.

As hard as Troy tried to push up and twist, he could not unseat the soldier, who had him pinned on the ground.

Troy decided there was only one thing left to try. He wriggled his way farther and farther under the soldier's seat, until the soldier's knees were near his armpits. Then Troy brought both of his legs up behind the soldier, and he wrapped them around either side of the soldier's head and neck. He then straightened his body out, pushing straight up in the air. He almost had to do a backward handstand to accomplish this because he was shorter than the soldier. He was able to force the soldier back. As Troy pushed up, he also twisted his body. As they both came down, Troy heard a snap. He had broken the soldier's neck.

Troy picked up Billy and continued until they were next to the old barn. He had to lay Billy on the ground to be able to pry the loose boards open. Billy's body was so weak from the venom that he had passed out. Troy had to crawl inside the barn first, and then lean back out to grab his buddy and drag him inside.

By this time, Brad had alerted the others that Troy and Billy were not in the bunker. They were preparing to search for the pair when Paisley announced she could see them on the cameras.

Brad and George went out to help Troy carry Billy inside the bunker.

Once safely inside, Troy showed the snake to Harold. No one in the bunker had seen that type of snake before. They guessed it might be some type of water snake.

"Judging from all the white inside its mouth, it could be a cottonmouth. But what would a cottonmouth be doing around this part of the country?" asked Darren.

Harold knew he didn't have any antivenin for nonlocal snakes. He also knew that sometimes antivenin could do more harm than good. It might save a person's life, but it could destroy inner organs as well. This boy was too young to take that chance, especially with no real hospitals around.

Troy's quick thinking to apply a splint to immobilize the leg and carry Billy back to the bunker may have saved Billy's life. Billy's leg had a huge swollen bubble just above his ankle. It looked like a huge, discolored water blister. Harold extracted as much of the poison as possible. He had Sue cleanse the area with soap. Harold then injected Billy with a tetanus vaccination.

If none of this helped, he knew that he might have to amputate Billy's leg. They would just have to watch, wait, see what happened, and do a lot of praying.

After Harold had taken over the care for Billy, Brad went in the social room and slumped in a chair. He placed his hands over his face and started to cry. There had been so much happening, and so suddenly, that no one noticed Debbie was not there.

Tasha was the first to ask. "Where's Mom?" she said.

Then she noticed her father in the chair. She knew something had happened. She went to Brad. She wanted to ask again where her mom was, but she couldn't get the words out. She knew her mom was dead.

After she finished straightening things up after the boys were brought in, Tonja noticed Brad and Tasha in the social area. She, too, could not speak. She had plenty of questions, but she could not say a word. She knew her mother was gone. Silence was the best thing for now.

Tonja sat with Brad and Tasha for a while. She knew her son would need her support also, so she rejoined Steve in their private area.

Troy went to Steve and Tonja. "It was my idea. I was going to be the hero and get us some fresh meat. Billy didn't want to go. I talked him into it.

"I had seen a deer in the camera monitors, but when we went out to get it, it was gone. So we followed the tracks. Oh, Dad, what we saw out there made us sick. It was...we saw..."

"I know, Son," Steve interrupted. "We saw all the devastation the last time we went out. That's how we know this Anthony Clemenz, the one who calls himself God, is really the Antichrist. That is why we told everyone to stay inside the bunker. Hopefully, if the soldiers come for us, they won't be able to get past our blast door and security measures."

Troy said, "That's part of what I'm trying to tell you." He hesitated but knew he had to tell it all. "I had to fight with a soldier to make it back here. I killed him, Dad. I didn't mean to, but when we were fighting, he got me pinned on the ground. I used that old Indian leghold that Uncle Jim taught me. When I brought him down to the ground, his neck broke.

"I know he was trying to kill me, but that doesn't make it any easier. I wanted to just sit and cry, but I had to get Billy back here to the doc. I'm so sorry. I never meant for all this to happen. I was just trying to get us some fresh meat...and now Billy is paying the price for my stupidity." Troy's eyes filled with tears that eventually started to make trails down his cheeks.

Steve tried to comfort his son. "The Lord knows why you went out there, Troy. We'll all pray for Billy. Between the Lord and Harold, I would say Billy stands a good chance of being okay."

After thinking for a moment, Steve asked, "What did you do with the soldier's body?"

Troy responded, "I wasn't sure what to do with him. I didn't have much time to think. Billy had already been bitten by that snake. I...just left him lying there."

"We'll have to keep a good watch on those monitors. You said you heard talking. That means he wasn't alone. The others will be looking for him, and after they find him, they'll be looking for us."

"Mom, you've been crying. Everything is okay now, isn't it?" asked Troy.

Tonja looked at Steve and Troy. The tears started to stream down her face again as she cried silently. "Mom is gone. She's dead. I don't know how yet. I'm sure Dad will fill us in later, when he can talk about it. For now, we just need to be there for him."

Troy gasped at the reality of what he had done. Because of him, everyone could be made to suffer. "Please, God, have mercy..." He prayed deep in his heart.

Things were quiet for a few days. The loss of Debbie hit home with everyone. Brad was finally able to talk about Debbie's death and what her final wishes were.

The family and friends seemed to grow even closer together from this great loss. They vowed to keep the Lord close in their hearts so that Clemenz would not win—not in their household.

Not the Final Chapter

Is This the End?

As Troy saw Billy enter the surveillance room, he brightened. "Good morning, Billy. It's so good to see you up and around." With sorrow in his heart, he continued, "I was so afraid I might have caused your death. I never could have lived with myself if you had died."

Billy understood the pain Troy was going through. "You know, while I was lying in bed, I was thinking how happy I was that it was me instead of you. If you had been bitten, neither of us would be here. I never could have carried you back. I never could have fought and won against that soldier. We would both be dead.

"And I don't want to hear any nonsense about it being your fault that we went out there. I wanted to go out there just as much as you did. I just don't have the courage to get up and do those kinds of things without you. You give me courage, and I thank you for that.

"Now let's not ever talk about this again. Agreed? Besides, we're starting to sound kind of syrupy."

Troy laughed at Billy's last remark. "Well, if you feel that way about it, I guess we could start deciding what our next prank will be."

Troy went back to monitoring the cameras. Billy pulled up a chair beside him. They sat quietly together. They were both alive and well now, so nothing more needed to be said.

It wasn't long before they noticed some soldiers sneaking around outside. The dead soldier's body had been found. The soldiers knew the bunker was there. They saw the sporadic drag marks Troy made when he carried Billy back to the barn.

All the soldiers had to do now was find the entrance to the bunker and figure out how to open it.

Troy called out, "Grandpa, the soldiers are here."

Brad went to the monitors to see exactly where the soldiers were and what they were doing. This would help him decide approximately how much time they would have to prepare.

Everyone scrambled to ready themselves for an attack. They moved those who could not help with the fighting into the soundproof room. It was the farthest area away from the main entrance, and it had the most camouflaged doorway inside the bunker. Those left in the room were given some weapons for self-protection in case they needed it.

Boxes and supplies were stacked in front of the door to try to hide it even more. This would allow a bit more safety for them, should the soldiers find a way to invade the bunker and overtake the first line of defense.

Everyone made sure their weapons were loaded, and they donned their bulletproof vests. They had to wait to see what would happen next.

Surprised at what he was witnessing, Troy called out, "Grandpa, you'd better take a look at this."

Brad returned to Troy's side. He looked at the security camera monitors in astonishment.

The sky had darkened. The clouds were starting to rumble and roll. It was as if a horrific storm was brewing. Hailstones started to fall. They looked like huge, white basketballs. Each stone must have weighed between twenty-five and fifty pounds.

The soldiers couldn't find any place to hide from the falling death.

Then the sky changed to a wonderment of colors like none had ever seen before. The sky was so brightly lit with blues, lavenders, reds, and oranges that it gave a feeling of spiritual warmth throughout the body.

As Brad drew in his breath, everyone gathered around to see what was happening.

Troy asked, "What does this mean, Grandpa?"

He expected his grandpa would know because he had read so many books, and he knew so much about the skies and stars.

Brad admitted, "I don't know, Troy. I have never seen or heard of anything like this ever happening before. I can't even make a suggestion for what this might be."

Troy continued to monitor the cameras.

The soldiers inside the barn got closer to finding the secret latch. One soldier called for the assistance of his commanding officer. He pointed in the general direction of the hidden latch. A flash of brilliant purple hit the man. The flash hit him so hard he flew out of the open side of the barn and into a tall hickory tree. His head was wedged in the crook between two branches. Other parts of his body dangled from different branches.

Troy wanted to turn his eyes away, but he couldn't. He was frozen. He watched as a flash of orange hit the ground. It was as if the sky was exploding. Brilliant fireballs were hurled everywhere. Fires started every time a ball hit against a tree, a person, or the ground.

The cameras blacked out as they melted from the heat the flash created.

The End Is Not Yet

Everyone in the bunker stopped in his tracks. They listened. They couldn't hear anything. Inside the bunker they would be safe from fire, radiation, and poisonous air. No one knew, however, if the bunker could withstand these brilliant fireballs being hurled from heaven. They would just have to sit and wait.

They waited for hours.

Hoping the soldiers would not be a threat to them anymore, they let everyone in the soundproof room out. They told them what had happened, but advised that they would have to be ready to move back in at a moment's notice.

Everyone in the bunker appeared to be safe. Nothing was able to damage or enter through the blast door or the vent's emergency shutdown system.

What had happened? Was it a freak storm? Had some type of bomb hit nearby? Could it have been both? It didn't matter what it was. They would have to stay shut in, until the outdoor air was fit to breathe again.

It took a couple of days for things to get back to normal. Soon, Troy and Billy were up to their old pranks. They put salt in the sugar bowl and sugar in the saltshaker.

They almost couldn't contain their laughter as Tonja and Cassie put what they thought was sugar in their coffees. The boys nudged the others to watch their victims' faces. Tonja happened to be facing the stove when she took her first sip of coffee, so only Cassie saw her reaction.

Cassie saw Tonja grimace at the taste of what she had just swallowed. Guessing what the boys had done, Cassie took a sip of her coffee and remarked, "Mmm, this is the best coffee I have ever tasted. We'll have to be stingy with this brand, so we don't run out so fast."

The boys, feeling a bit foiled in their efforts to pull off a good prank, waited for Tonja and Cassie to make breakfast. It was the morning to have eggs, so they figured they might have some success yet.

Everyone sat down for breakfast. The first one to be served eggs was Brad. He took one bite. The shock of the surprisingly sweet eggs made Brad spit the food right back out. He spit it out so quickly, and with such force, that it landed right in Troy's face.

The boys got their wish. Everyone had a good, hardy laugh. That included Troy, after the shock wore off.

A couple of months had passed since the group had become completely shut-in. Jules and Diti were becoming closer and closer. Where one was, the other one was, too. They helped each other do their chores. They played games together. Diti even helped Paisley with the girlie things she had to do.

The End Is Not Yet

Together they approached Steve and Tonja.

Jules started the conversation. "Mom, Dad, we would like you to be the first to know. We would like to get married. This might not seem like the proper time, but we love each other. And for now, at least, life is moving on. There isn't any preacher here, so we were wondering if you would perform the ceremony for us."

Steve and Tonja looked at each other. Then Steve responded, "We think this is a great idea. We all need a real reason to celebrate, and what better reason could there be than a wedding? We are honored you have asked us to be part of your great day. When would you like this to happen?"

Diti answered, "Well, we understand you will need some time to prepare for this, so..." She hesitated and giggled. "How about tomorrow?"

"I guess you won't be letting any grass grow under your feet!" Tonja gave a slight laugh. "We'll start the preparations right away. Go ahead and make your announcement. I'm sure everyone will appreciate the vast amount of time you've given them to prepare."

The rest of the day was used to prepare a fine wedding. Everyone took turns in the shower. The girls curled each other's hair. They pulled out the fanciest clothes they could find, and made sure that each item was pressed perfectly. Cassie baked and decorated a cake. She had to use dried fruit to decorate it, but it turned out to be one of the nicest cakes she had ever made. Others drifted off into corners, together or alone, to make gifts for the newlywed couple.

The next morning, everyone awoke early with happy expectations of the day's events. The morning went smoothly, with all the necessary last-minute finishes. Tonja, Tasha, and Cassie decided what to make for a special meal.

"I've got it," announced Tonja. "We can make some macaroni and cheese. Everyone loves macaroni and cheese, especially Jules."

"We should try to make it special somehow. We'd have to make it with powdered milk and powdered cheese. That might be kind of bland," Cassie said.

"We still have some dehydrated ham, onions, and mushrooms, don't we?" inquired Tasha. "That stuff always tastes good together."

They each wanted to put a personal twist on it. When Cassie and Tasha weren't looking, Tonja sprinkled her favorite seasoning into the mixture. Then, when Tonja and Cassie weren't looking, Tasha sprinkled in her favorite seasoning. Finally, when Cassie got her chance, she secretly sprinkled her favorite seasoning into the dish.

When the macaroni and cheese was finally served, it was the tastiest meal everyone had eaten in a long time, but they would never have been able to duplicate it. No one would divulge what she had done to doctor up the macaroni and cheese. Each of them secretly smiled and thought she alone had been the one to save the day.

Sue found some loose, old gauze that she wouldn't be able to use as bandages. She and Rosie made it into a wedding veil for Diti.

"How could she be a bride without a veil to cover her face until the right moment?" Sue said.

Diti cried tears of joy and thankfulness when Sue and Rosie presented the veil to her.

Tasha approached Diti after Sue gave her the veil. "Okay, that is something new. What do we have that is blue?"

Tonja pulled a pair of blue sapphire earrings out of her pocket. She was waiting for just this moment to give them to Diti.

"And here is something borrowed." Tasha had a pin that Debbie's mother had given to Debbie. The pin had been given to Debbie's mother by Debbie's grandmother on her eighteenth birthday in 1933. "I'm sure Great-Grandma would be so proud to have you borrow this today," Tasha said.

Together, Brad and Tonja took Jules to the side. Brad had taken a ring out of Debbie's jewelry box. It would be perfect for the marriage of two people who really loved each other. They gave the ring to Jules so he would have a ring to put on Diti's finger.

Between Darren, Troy, and Billy, someone came up with the idea of placing some plastic sheeting, tinfoil, Bubble Wrap, and anything else they could find that would make noise under the sheets of the newlyweds' bed.

The ceremony started and finished, and then it was time for everyone to go to bed.

"I...excuse me," Brad started to say. "Steve and I have an extra surprise for the newlywed couple."

Steve walked over and opened the door at the far end of the bunker. The two of them had snuck off when everyone else was busy with their own little projects, and they had set up the perfect little love nest in the soundproof room. It had scented candles and a digital music player with romantic music in it. All it needed was for the two lovebirds to finish the scene.

Brad continued, "Rest assured, you will have your privacy this evening."

Troy turned to Darren. Seeming a little down in the mouth, he said, "I guess we can go clean out all that stuff we put in their bed now."

The day had been so full of fun and laughter that they almost forgot they were enclosed in a bunker for an unknown amount of time. Today none of that mattered to anyone.

To be on the safe side, they stayed in the bunker for three months.

The End Is Not Yet

They had plenty of food and water, so they just waited to see what would happen next. As far as they knew, there wasn't any food or water to be had outside.

They didn't know if the air would be safe outside, and they didn't want to take the chance of letting bad air in while setting new sensors outside. The original sensors had melted like the cameras during the flash storm.

When it seemed like the time was right, Brad took a new sensor and placed it in front of a small plate they had rigged in the door when they built the bunker. The plate could be slid to the side just far enough to push a sensor through it.

He taped some clear plastic over the plate and the sensor. He left the plastic loose enough to work with it, slide the plate to the side, and maneuver the sensor through the opening without letting any air inside the bunker. They could then take a quick reading of the air outside.

They gave the sensor time to get acclimated and then read the meter. Brad sighed at the results. The air was good. In fact, the air was great. They could now venture outside.

As everyone came out of the bunker, they were torn about how to react. The land was so devastated, but the feeling of the fresh, clean air was so new.

It was a different world. Everything had been

destroyed. Whatever was aboveground was no more, but all the signs of death had been burned up and washed away. The rivers that once had flowed with so much blood ran clear again. The lake was clean. It was as if all the bad had been swept away.

The soldiers were gone. They had been so intent on finding the bunker people that they had forgotten to watch the heavens.

This was the first time some of them had been outdoors in years. They enjoyed the deep breaths of fresh air that filled their lungs. It felt as if the sun was not needed to make it warm or light. Yet the warmth and the light were all around them.

Tonja and Tasha gave their husbands a hug and a kiss. Feeling the need to be by their father, they stepped toward him. With one on each side, they placed each placed an arm around him.

Feeling the joy of all this, Brad said, "If we made it through this, others must have made it also. We'll go over to Fred's to advise them the air is clear, just in case they don't know it yet."

Tasha leaned her head on Brad's shoulder. Looking at the ground around them, she said, "Do you see the tiny sprigs of grass peeping up over there?"

Their love for the Lord had seen them through, but the end was not yet.

The End Is Not Yet

Suddenly everyone's attention was drawn toward the sky. Off in the distance, a heavenly blue cloud was descending to earth. As it got closer, it became brighter and whiter. It was Christ on a white horse.

As the Lord slowly descended closer to earth, the clouds behind him became more visible. Soon, souls standing on those clouds became visible. They were waving, smiling, and giving cheers of love for those still alive on the ground.

As the souls become more visible, some of the faces became distinguishable. Justin's smiling face appeared. As they continued to look upon the souls, Tasha and Tonja were the first to see her. Then Brad's face lit up as he watched his beloved Debbie move from behind some of the other souls. She waved to him. There was a glistening coming from her eyes. One would think they were tears of joy, but they were not tears. It was the glistening warmth of love. They would be together again. Indeed, the end was not yet!

Not taking his eyes off Debbie, Brad said to his daughters, "I never knew why, but all my life there has been a scripture from 1 Thessalonians in my heart. It says, 'Then we who are alive *and* remain shall be caught up together with them in the clouds to meet the Lord in the air. And thus we shall always be with the Lord. Therefore comfort one another with these words.' Now I know why."

Scriptures

from

The King James Version of the Holy Bible

Romans 3:23

Romans 12:19–21

1 Thessalonians 4:17–18

2 Thessalonians 2:3

2 Timothy 3:1–5

2 Peter 3:3–4

Revelation 2:10–11

Revelation 3:15, 16

Revelation 3:20, 21

Revelation 6:15

Revelation 11:1–2

Revelation 11:3–14

Revelation 13:2–3, 5, 7

Revelation 13:10

Revelation 13:16–18

Revelation 16:21

Revelation 21:23

Revelation 22:5

Diane Pillars worked as a heavy equipment operator before retiring as a sergeant from the Alaska Department of Corrections. A licensed cosmetologist for over thirty-five years, she is also the first lady exalted ruler and first lady district deputy grand exalted ruler for the Alaskan Benevolent and Protective Order of Elks.

An avid volunteer, Pillars has received numerous accolades, including the volunteer of the year award from the Mat-Su Council on the Prevention of Alcoholism and Drug Abuse, and a member of the year award from the Alaska Peace Officers Association.

Pillars is a proud wife, mother, grandmother, and great-grandmother.